South ... Public Library

W9-ARB-872

"Addy," he said, "this isn't going to change anything."

"Not for you," she allowed. "But it will for me."

"What are you doing?" he demanded as Addy pulled his wheelchair toward the door.

"Taking you out onto the porch," she replied.

The second the warmth of the afternoon sun lit upon his face, Jake felt better. It had been days since he'd been outside.

Pleasure gave way to the pain of his past. The shock. The fervent prayers. The guilt.

"Jake…" A gentle hand came to rest on his arm.

Opening his eyes, he drank in Addy's pretty face and the unspoken comfort her gentle touch offered.

"Are you okay? If being out here is too much…"

He shook his head. "No, I'm fine. I just forgot how good the sun's warmth could feel." Being with her felt good, too. Odd how he could be so angry with Addy yet be calmed by her presence.

Did she still fill a small piece of his heart?

NOV 0 0 2021

Kat Brookes is a multipublished, award-winning author. She has been married to her childhood sweetheart, the love of her life, for over thirty years. They've been blessed with two beautiful daughters and an adorable Australian shepherd named Mac. She loves writing stories that can both make you smile and touch your heart. Kat is represented by Michelle Grajkowski with 3 Seas Literary Agency. Read more about Kat and her upcoming releases at katbrookes.com. Email her at katbrookes@comcast.net, or contact her on Facebook at katbrookes.

Books by Kat Brookes

Love Inspired

Small Town Sisterhood

With All Her Heart
The Missionary's Purpose

Bent Creek Blessings

The Cowboy's Little Girl
The Rancher's Baby Surprise
Hometown Christmas Gift

Texas Sweethearts

Her Texas Hero
His Holiday Matchmaker
Their Second Chance Love

Visit the Author Profile page at Harlequin.com.

The Missionary's Purpose

Kat Brookes

LOVE INSPIRED

INSPIRATIONAL ROMANCE

If you purchased this book without a cover you should be aware that this book is stolen property. It was reported as "unsold and destroyed" to the publisher, and neither the author nor the publisher has received any payment for this "stripped book."

LOVE INSPIRED®
INSPIRATIONAL ROMANCE

Recycling programs
for this product may
not exist in your area.

ISBN-13: 978-1-335-56716-1

The Missionary's Purpose

Copyright © 2021 by Kimberly Duffy

All rights reserved. No part of this book may be used or reproduced in any manner whatsoever without written permission except in the case of brief quotations embodied in critical articles and reviews.

This is a work of fiction. Names, characters, places and incidents are either the product of the author's imagination or are used fictitiously. Any resemblance to actual persons, living or dead, businesses, companies, events or locales is entirely coincidental.

This edition published by arrangement with Harlequin Books S.A.

For questions and comments about the quality of this book, please contact us at CustomerService@Harlequin.com.

Love Inspired
22 Adelaide St. West, 40th Floor
Toronto, Ontario M5H 4E3, Canada
www.Harlequin.com

Printed in U.S.A.

The Lord is my strength and my shield;
my heart trusted in him, and I am helped:
therefore my heart greatly rejoiceth;
and with my song will I praise him.
—*Psalms* 28:7

I'd like to dedicate this book
to my own real-life hero, Ron.
He is a kind, caring, unfailingly supportive man.
He doesn't hesitate to help others when called
upon. He finds ways to help those in need without
ever taking credit for it. And like Jake, who
believed in Addy and helped her to realize her
dream, my husband has done the same for me
in my pursuit of becoming, and continuing on as,
a published author. I love him for
supporting me, for motivating me, for being
the perfect example of what a true hero really is.

Chapter One

"Aunt Addy!"

Addy smiled as her foster sister's son, Finn, came racing toward her. Opening her arms wide, she accepted the nine-year-old's warm, welcoming hug. Needing it more than she had realized until that very moment. She'd spent the drive back to Sweet Springs and Mama Tully mulling over her current job situation. Or jobless situation, as was her case.

Days earlier, Addy had learned her position as head pastry chef for a privately owned hotel had been terminated. A larger chain had bought out the hotel and was bringing in its own staff. That meant her time back in Sweet Springs was not only going to be spent visiting with her foster mother, Mama Tully, and helping Lila with preparations for her upcoming wedding to Mason Landers. She would also spend it searching job listings for her chosen career in the Atlanta metro area. Maybe beyond that area, as jobs in her field weren't all that plentiful. The thought of starting over again career-wise was daunting. Not that she'd have to begin at the bottom. She was good at what she did, had years of professional experience behind her. It was more the thought of forming new professional relationships, workplace friendships, when her past had left her more guarded when it came to those things. But she would push through and find a spot for herself once again.

"Well," she said, giving Finn one more affectionate squeeze before releasing him, "if it isn't my little sweetie pie, Finn Gleeson."

"Not for much longer," he replied excitedly as she set him back down onto his feet.

She looked down at him with a tender smile. "I like you just the size you are, but even when you grow to be big and strong, you're still going to be my little sweetie pie," she teased, giving the dark curls at the top of his head a playful tussle. She knew full well Finn wasn't referring to his height when he'd said not much longer, but she wanted it to be his news to tell.

"I'm not talking about growing bigger," he said, shaking his head.

"You're not?" Oh, how she adored this little boy. One she had helped Lila to raise for the first few precious years of his life, until he and Lila had moved from Atlanta to Alabama. While she and Lila had talked often since her best friend and foster sister moved back to Sweet Springs, it was actually seeing the true happiness on both her and Finn's faces that told Addy happily-ever-afters really did exist. But did they for everyone?

"Didn't Momma tell you?" he asked. "I'm getting my daddy's name! I'm going to be a Landers!"

"You are?" she said, feigning surprise. He was referring to the changes Lila was having made to her son's birth certificate.

His head bobbed up and down. "Yep. I get to be Finn Landers!"

She would never forget the day her foster sister, only seventeen at the time, had shown up on Addy's family's doorstep, pregnant and distraught over the decision she'd made to run off from Sweet Springs. Addy had made a promise that day to keep Finn's existence a secret. It hadn't been easy keeping the truth from Mama Tully and Mrs. Landers. Two very special women who had so graciously taken her under their motherly wings, showing her nothing but kindness and love. It felt like such a betrayal to them both, but just as Lila had her reasons for leaving Sweet Springs without telling Mason about the baby, Addy had her own for keeping Lila's secret. She'd feared Lila running off again and ending up living on the streets like Addy and her momma had for so many years.

"It does have a good ring to it," Addy agreed, forcing her smile to remain intact.

The door to the old Victorian that had once been their foster home flew open. "Addy!" Lila exclaimed and flew across the porch with Mama Tully right on her heels.

They embraced, squeezing each other tight.

"Why didn't you call to tell us you were coming?" Lila asked with a bright smile. "I would have had Finn moved out of your room and had your linens washed before you got here."

If she had told Lila over the phone about the loss of her job, Lila would have spent time worrying over her. "I wanted to surprise you," Addy said. It was also because she'd needed to prepare herself mentally. Returning to Sweet Springs meant facing those she'd hurt by having kept Lila's secret all those years. She would take a day or two to mend her relationship with Mama Tully before doing the same with the Landers. "And I'm good with sleeping on the couch for a night or two."

"Well, you certainly did surprise us," Mama Tully said as she joined them. "And it won't take any time at all to get Finn moved in with Lila." Her expression softened, and she spread her arms wide. "Welcome home, Addy."

Addy smiled, a sheen of tears filling her eyes. "Mama Tully." She stepped forward into the embrace of the woman who had taken on the role of mother to a disenchanted young teen who had only seen the harsher side of life. A girl who had learned how to become a survivor the hard way, having spent part of her childhood on the streets of Atlanta, living in a beat-up old car with her momma. Her daddy, not a family kind of man, had taken off the moment he'd learned her momma was with child. When Addy was little, life had taught her to trust her instincts when it came to survival, and to always be strong no matter how scared she might be inside. Then, at thirteen, after child services had taken her from her momma because of her inability to provide a stable home for Addy, she'd been placed with Mama Tully, who had shown her what it was like to feel safe, to be able to trust in others, to trust in the Lord when times were hard. She had shown her there was more than one path to choose to travel in life. If not for Mama Tully and Mrs. Landers, her neighbor and close friend, helping to guide Addy, believing in her, she had no idea where she might have ended up in her life. Certainly not working in a field where she got paid to do what she loved. It was Mrs. Landers who had helped Addy discover her passion for baking, helping to pave her way to a career she loved. And how had she repaid her? By keeping Finn's existence from her all those years. She didn't deserve Mrs. Landers's forgiveness, but she'd received it all the same.

"Let me take a look at you," Mama Tully said, taking a step back. "You're still as pretty as ever."

While Lila hadn't spoken to anyone after leaving Sweet Springs until returning recently Addy had remained in contact with Mama Tully and the Landers family, mostly over the phone. Her job kept her too busy to do much traveling, but more than that kept Addy from coming back as often as she might have liked to. It was the guilt of keeping Lila's secret from those she cared about, the fear of letting something slip. She missed her occasional visits back to Sweet Springs so very much. It had been a hurt she'd learned to live with for Lila's sake.

When the truth finally had come out that past summer, Addy had made her own heartfelt apologies to all involved. Everyone had eventually expressed forgiveness—except for Mason's younger brother, Jake. Addy had built a special friendship with him through their many phone conversations and her occasional visits over the years. She mourned the loss of their bond more than she would have ever thought possible. If he weren't away on a mission trip, one he'd gone on in Mason's place so that his brother could remain in Sweet Springs with Lila and his son, she would have sought him out. Done whatever she could to earn his forgiveness and rebuild their friendship.

"Addy?" Lila prompted.

Mentally shoving her troubled thoughts aside, she said lightheartedly, "The wonders of makeup." But it was true. Between the few fine lines that being almost thirty brought and the shadows beneath her eyes that came from several sleepless nights mulling over her future, she needed all the help she could get.

"And you've cut your hair."

"It was time for my long hair to go." She reached up to touch the dark, shoulder-length strands. "It's an A-line bob. Shorter in the back, longer in the front."

"It looks lovely on you, honey."

"I agree," Lila said. "It really goes well with the shape of your face."

"Thank you," she told them. "Mama Tully, you look wonderful. How are you feeling?"

"She has more energy than I do," Lila said.

"I was so weak from being in that hospital and during my recovery afterward," Mama Tully explained. "I don't ever want to feel that way again. So I intend to keep moving and doing whatever it takes to keep my body strong."

"I'm so sorry I wasn't able to make it here to be with you sooner," Addy said with an apologetic frown. To think of all the time she'd wasted hiring and then training an assistant to cover for her, only to end up not having a job at all.

"I know you would have been here if you could have been. Not to worry. I was in good hands," Mama Tully assured her, looking to Lila and Finn.

"My daddy helped, too," Finn stated proudly.

"Yes, he did," Mama Tully agreed. "Now grab your suitcase and we'll take this reunion inside. I'll pour us some sweet tea to sip on while we catch up."

"Suitcases," Addy clarified with an apologetic smile. "I'll be staying longer than I had originally planned to. That is, if it's okay with you, Mama Tully."

She scoffed. "As if I'd have any objection to your staying on longer."

"I'm so happy to be able to spend more time with you and Lila and Finn. And I'll be able to help Lila with anything and everything she still needs help with for the wedding." She looked to her friend. "Your big day is going to be here before you know it."

"Um… Addy," Lila began uneasily, something very akin to worry replacing her warm smile, "there's been a change of plans for the wedding. I was going to call to let you know, but Mason and I are still ironing out the details."

"The wedding's still on, though?" She looked from Lila to Mama Tully, trying to read their expressions. What she saw there was masked unease.

"We've decided to push the wedding back until spring," Lila explained.

"So Uncle Jake will be out of his wheelchair and can dance, too," Finn happily supplied.

Addy's heart gave a start at his words. She whipped her gaze back to Lila. "Out of his wheelchair?" she said in what came out as a panicked demand.

Her friend frowned. "Jake encountered a bit of trouble while he was building that schoolhouse in the Republic of Congo."

Addy felt her heart pounding in her chest. "What kind of trouble?" she asked, not sure if she really wanted to hear the answer. The thought of Jake having an accident serious enough to land him in a wheelchair was almost too much for her to bear.

"He got shot," Finn said matter-of-factly.

"Finn," Lila said in gentle warning.

"Shot?" Addy croaked, her hand flying to her mouth. That went far beyond her imagining.

"And broke his leg," Finn added with a nod, clearly not picking up on his mother's desire for him to remain silent on the matter.

"Jake was shot?" Addy replied, shock at the news muddling her thoughts.

"He's going to be okay," Mama Tully said, giving Addy a soothing pat on the arm.

Lila nodded. "The doctor expects him to make a complete recovery physically."

Physically? Why did that word have to stick out like a sore thumb? Then another word shoved that one aside. *Shot.* Addy glanced worriedly in the direction of the Landers place, which lay just beyond the orchard that lined Mama Tully's side yard.

"When did it happen?" Addy asked, the words pinched with emotion. *How? Why?* The fearful questions swarmed about inside her head. Ones she refrained from asking with Finn within hearing range. *Oh, Jake.*

"Finn, honey," Mama Tully said, "why don't you and I carry some of your aunt Addy's things into the house for her and start getting her room ready for her stay here?"

"Okay," he replied. "What do you want me to carry?"

Addy attempted to shake free of the surprise that filled her. "You can be in charge of carrying Peaches inside."

"You brought Peaches?" he exclaimed.

"I thought she might like a vacation, too," she answered. "And your Gramma Tully said it was all right to bring her."

"She's my grandkitty," her foster mother said. "Of course she's welcome to stay here, too. What would you like me to carry in for you?"

"There are only two suitcases and a carry-on. Lila and I can get those," she told her. One had her clothes, the other the gift she'd bought for Lila and Mason along with crafting supplies for making wedding favors.

"If you're sure," Mama Tully replied.

"I am. Finn can carry Peaches in," Addy said, forcing her gaze not to drift off toward the orchard. "He looks strong enough for the task." The very thought that Jake had been shot had her stomach twisting in knots. It was made even worse that things were still so strained between them. When she'd last seen Jake the prior fall, they'd had so much fun together. Even during their phone calls, they were constantly laughing, thoroughly enjoying each other's company. Until Jake had found out about her part in keeping Finn's existence from his family. She understood his anger. Accepted it. That didn't make the news of his having been hurt any easier. She couldn't bear the thought they might never laugh together again.

"I am," Lila's son said, drawing Addy back to the moment.

She looked over to see Finn flexing his currently nonexistent muscles in demonstration.

Laughing softly, Mama Tully said, "I'll go on ahead into the house and put Honey and Grits in their room until they've had a chance to be introduced to Peaches."

"If it ends up being a problem having Peaches here—"

Her foster mother waved a hand of dismissal, cutting Addy off. "Don't even think it. They're going to love her. Honey and Grits are quite fond of the Landerses' barn cats. So now that that's settled, I'll go prepare them for meeting their new friend." Turning, Mama Tully scurried away toward the house.

Addy hoped her foster mother was right. That settling in wouldn't be too much of a challenge for her sweet kitty or for the pups.

Lila moved to stand beside her. "They'll be fine," she said assuredly, clearly having read Addy's troubled thoughts. "Those dogs are the biggest, sweetest four-legged babies I've ever met. Peaches will have them wrapped right around her little paws in no time at all."

Addy might have smiled at that if she wasn't so consumed with worry over Jake. "Peaches is in her carrier in the back seat if you want to go get her for me," she told Finn.

"Sure," he said with a nod before racing off in the direction of her car, where he wasted no time in retrieving the bright pink travel carrier. "I've missed you," he cooed to the meowing cat inside as he made his way back past Addy and Lila. "Wait until you meet Gramma Tully. She gives lots and lots of hugs and kisses."

As soon as he was out of earshot, Addy

turned to Lila. "Be honest. How is Jake really? Who shot him? How bad is it?"

"Shhh..." Lila said in a calming voice. "I hate seeing you so worked up. Not that I don't understand your reaction to the news about Jake."

"News I should have been told about. You know how close we are...er, *were*," Addy corrected with a deepening frown. "Despite his cutting me out of his life, I still care about Jake."

"I know you do," Addy agreed. "And I decided to wait to tell you once you got here. Otherwise you would have hopped in your car the moment you found out and drove here in a far too distracted state of mind."

Her sister knew her well. "Then tell me now," she pleaded. "What happened?"

"Guerrillas ambushed Jake's missionary group while they were building the new schoolhouse. I don't have all the details, as Jake isn't up to talking about it, but..."

"But what?" Addy demanded, her heart pounding furiously in her chest.

Frowning, Lila said, "He's having a rough time dealing with everything that happened. We're not sure how to go about helping him through this ordeal since he refuses to talk about it. All we know is the mission workers who were building the new school were ambushed and that Jake took a bullet to the shoulder during the melee. Apparently, he was coming down a ladder when he was shot, causing him to fall and break his leg."

"Oh Jake," Addy breathed, imagining the fear and pain he must have felt. "I have to see him," she said, heart pounding. Turning away, she took off toward her car.

"Addy!" Lila called after her.

"I won't be long. I just need to know that he's okay!" she called back over her shoulder as she slid behind the wheel of her car, tears blurring her vision. Starting the engine, she threw the car into gear and drove off.

"Addy?" Mrs. Landers said in surprise when she opened the door. She looked tired, her shoulders drawn in and crescent-moon shadows stretched beneath her dark eyes. Her shoulder-length hair was pulled up into a messy bun, with several random strands having worked their way free to stick out in disarray.

"Hello," she greeted, trying not to show the trepidation that filled her. "I just got to Mama Tully's. Lila told me about Jake," she said, unable to keep her voice from cracking. "May I see him?"

Mrs. Landers frowned. "I'm not sure this is a good time for a visit. Jake's not quite himself right now."

Who would be, after going through what he had? "I'm sorry. I should never have come over unannounced like I did. But when Lila told me Jake had been injured—"

A banging sounded in the nearby hallway, causing Addy to fall silent as her and Mrs. Landers's gazes moved in that direction. The front of a wheelchair, one of its footrests lifted to elevate Jake's casted leg, protruded from a doorway. A second later, he maneuvered it into the hallway.

"Jake," his momma gasped, surprise lighting her face. "You're up."

He looked more exhausted than his momma, yet Addy didn't miss the spark of fury that lit his dark eyes as he glowered in her direction. He struggled to turn his chair so that he could fully face the front entryway.

Mrs. Landers hurried to help him.

"I can do it," he muttered in frustration.

"You're not supposed to be using your injured arm," she gently reminded her son. She moved behind him to turn the chair and push him into the entryway, where Addy stood watching uneasily.

"I can't believe you let her into our house,"

he said and then directed his attention at Addy. "Why are you here?" he demanded of her.

Because I care about you. Because I've missed talking to you. Addy couldn't speak past the pain of his rejection. Not that she hadn't expected it, but it hurt deeply all the same.

"Jake," Mrs. Landers scolded, "that's not how I raised you. And it seems pretty clear to me why she's here. The Good Lord sent Addy to us."

The Good Lord? Addy stood dumbstruck. Wherever had Jake's momma gotten that idea from? She and the Lord had parted ways a long time ago, making her one of the last people He'd be sending anywhere.

Jake glanced up over his shoulder, certain he'd misheard his momma. Maybe it was due to exhaustion, because as much time as he'd spent shut away in his room, it hadn't been in peaceful slumber. Or maybe he could write it off as the pain medicine. Not that he took it as often as he probably ought to. He needed to feel the agony. Deserved to feel it. If it hadn't been for him, Corey, his fellow missionary and newfound friend, might still be alive. He'd traded places with Corey to go grab them a couple of bottles of water. He was just going down the rungs of the scaffolding ladder when the shooting began. His friend took the fatal bullet that should have struck Jake instead.

"What?" Jake croaked out in response to his momma's comment as he shoved the unwanted memories away.

She smiled tiredly as she rounded the wheelchair to stand next to him. "I said that Addy's presence here could only be divine intervention."

He looked to Addy, who had betrayed their whole family, and then back to his momma. "How on earth do you figure that?"

"Because you've barely left your room, or uttered a word, since you've been home," she calmly explained. "Over a week now. And then Addy shows up, and you're out of your room and talking."

"I came out of my room because I couldn't believe my ears," he muttered. "Why would ever you let *her*, of all people, into our house?"

"Because there is a doormat right outside that front door, one you bought me for Mother's Day last year, that reads, Welcome to Our Home."

Jake dragged a hand down over his face, releasing a heavy sigh of frustration. He didn't want to "welcome" Addy. Shouldn't even have to. Not after she'd wronged his family. Wronged him. Made him cherish their friendship. One that had been built around a lie. "I never meant to cause any trouble," Addy said, her gaze misting over. "I just needed to know that Jake was all right."

"Your concern is appreciated," his momma told her. "In fact, I'm grateful you stopped by."

Addy's eyes widened. "You are?"

"You've done what none of his family has been able to do," his momma replied. "Spark some life back into my son, and I thank you for that from the bottom of my heart."

"Addy had nothing to do with…" He let the words trail off. Maybe she had been the catalyst for his motivation to leave his room, but only because his momma seemed to have suffered a momentary loss of memory. Addy had spent the past nine years pretending to be their friend, *his* friend, when all the while she was keeping the truth about Mason having a son from all of them.

"I'm so happy you're up and about," his momma told him. "But I'm just plain worn out." She looked to Addy. "Since you came over to look in on Jake, would you mind keeping my son company while I go lie down for a spell? A half an hour at the most, as I have pies cooling in the kitchen that I'll need to see to."

"That's not going to hap—"

"Happy," Addy blurted out, cutting his refusal off. "I mean I would be more than happy to visit with Jake while you rest."

"Thank you, honey." Before Jake could utter another word, his momma turned and walked away. She had looked tired, no doubt thanks to the time she'd spent caring for him since his return home, but to abandon him to Addy...

His hands curled around the oversize wheels on either side of him. "I don't need anyone keeping me company," he mumbled in frustration, then attempted to wheel away, but his right arm refused to cooperate fully. All he succeeded in doing was spinning in a half circle.

"Especially me," she said with a sigh. "I know. But if you care about your momma, you'll make an exception just this once. I've never seen her look so worn out."

His momma had been burning the candle at both ends. She spent hours baking for, and working at, The Perfect Peach, their family market, while helping Lila prepare for her wedding to Mason. One they had only recently postponed because of him. And now his momma was spending every free moment she had seeing to his care. He'd insisted he didn't need someone watching over him, especially some stranger hired on to look after him, nurse or not. But his family was lovingly persistent if anything and determined to see to his needs, all the same.

Getting back to his room on his own would be a challenge to say the least. He'd learned that the hard way, determined to do things on his own and discovering his body wasn't even close to being ready to get back to life the way it was. And to be stubborn now, because it was Addy offering to help, could mean exacerbating the injury to his slowly healing shoulder. With a resigned sigh, he said, "You've got a half hour, but I can't promise I'm going to be in a talkative mood." He'd much rather be shut away in his room, as he had been since coming back from Africa, surfing the internet on his phone or reading one of the many books he had on modernizing fruit orchards.

Moving around behind him, Addy grabbed a hold of the chair's handle grips.

He twisted around and then winced at the sharp stabbing in his shoulder. "What do you think you're doing?"

Her gaze dropped to the white gauze sticking out from underneath the opening of his shirt collar. Her expression looked as pained as his shoulder felt at that moment. "Jake," she gasped. "Your momma is worried enough about you without you tearing your stitches, or whatever they had to use to close your wound."

He acknowledged that with a nod and then eased back around to face the door, his arms coming to rest atop the wheelchair's padded armrests.

"Look," she said, "I know I'm the last person you want to talk to, but I really need to talk to you. You don't have to say a thing. Just hear me out."

"Addy," he said tiredly, "this isn't going to change anything."

"Not for you," she allowed. "But it will for me."

"What are you doing?" he demanded as Addy spun him around to face the hallway. A second later, she was pulling the chair backward toward the front door.

"Taking you out onto the porch for some sunshine and fresh air," she replied. Opening the door, she nudged it open and pulled the chair out onto the porch with her. "It sounds like you can use a little of both."

The second the warmth of the afternoon sun lit upon his face, Jake had to bite back a groan of pleasure. It had been days since he'd been outside. Closing his eyes, he inhaled deeply, taking in the familiar scents of fall, damp earth and the scent of nearby campfires. He could pick up the faint aroma of freshly baked peach pies. All those familiar smells of home. A place he'd feared he might never see again when the gunfire had erupted, and screams rose up around him, that day in the Congo.

His moment of pleasure gave way to the pain of his past. The shock. The fervent prayers. And then the guilt.

"Jake…" A gentle hand came to rest on his arm.

Opening his eyes, he looked up, drinking in Addy's pretty face and the unspoken comfort her gentle touch offered. He felt the tension ease out of his chest.

"You cut your hair," he stated.

"I did," she said.

"It looks good."

She smiled as if the remark had given her heart a little jolt of pleasure. "Thank you."

Not wanting to think about her response, because she hadn't cared about his family's happiness, Jake leaned his head back and closed his eyes. The moment the sun touched upon his face, he let out a low groan.

"Jake? Are you okay? " Addy asked worriedly. "If being out here is too much for you…"

He shook his head. "No, I'm fine. I just forgot how good the sun's warmth could feel." Being with her felt good, too. Odd how he could be so angry with Addy, yet at the same time he was somehow calmed by her presence. Maybe she still filled a small piece of his heart. Not that Addy had ever known she'd held it. She thought of him as a friend. As Mason's little brother. And while their age difference had once mattered, they were adults now. Had been for a very long while. Besides, Addy was only twenty-nine. Three scant years older than he himself was. It ended up being a good thing he'd been waiting for Addy to give him some sign that she reciprocated his growing feelings before confessing his own, because he would have been made to look a fool. One didn't lie to those they truly cared about.

"You look a little pale."

Addy's voice pulled Jake's focus back to her. "All the more reason to sit out here for a little while," he said, opening his eyes to look up at her.

"Then let's give you a better view." She positioned his chair a few inches back, then set the wheel locks. Once that was done, she lowered herself to sit on the edge of the porch. "Jake," she began, "I know you hate me…"

"*Hate*'s a pretty strong word," he countered. But so very close to what he'd felt inside when he'd learned of her part in keeping Finn from his family for all those years.

"Whatever you want to call it, you've shut me out of your life," she told him, and he heard the hurt in her voice.

"Addy, you lied to me. To all my family for years," he reminded her. "How am I supposed to get past that?" Even if the rest of his family had.

She sighed softly. "I can't answer that for you. All I can do is tell you how sorry I am for hurting you the way I did. That's the last thing I ever wanted to do."

His gaze locked with hers. "But you had to know that's exactly what your keeping Lila's secret would do. I thought you and I…" He looked away.

"I gave my word to Lila," she told him. "For so many reasons, I had to keep the promise I made to her. I still care about you. Losing your friendship is tearing me apart." Tears filled her eyes, something one rarely saw with

Addy, and, as much as Jake hated allowing it to do so, it pulled at his heartstrings. "It's going to be so hard being in Sweet Springs and knowing I can't be a part of your life."

Friendship. It had been so much more than that to him. *Had* been. And Addy wasn't the only one torn apart over the ramifications of her betrayal. "I've learned the hard way," he said, motioning to the cast on his lower leg, "that life doesn't always go the way we expect it to. All we can do is try to pick ourselves up and move on." Just as he would find a way to do.

The front screen door creaked open, drawing their gazes in that direction.

His momma stepped outside to join them on the porch. "I couldn't sleep, so I thought I might as well come out here and relieve Addy. I'm sure she's anxious to get back to Vera's since she came right over as soon as she heard about you." She looked to Addy. "Thank you for keeping Jake company."

"I was happy to do it," Addy replied as she rose from her perch on the steps. Turning to Jake, she said determinedly, "I'm not giving up on our friendship. It means far too much to me." That said, she descended the steps and headed for her car.

Jake watched her go, thinking he should

warn her that she'd only be wasting her time. But the breath to speak those words refused to depart his lungs. He wanted to blame it on his weakened state, but he knew that would be a lie. The emotional response he'd had to seeing Addy again proved that while his head had, his heart hadn't completely set her aside.

Chapter Two

Addy had been home for three days and still couldn't get the memory of Jake in that wheelchair out of her mind. It had been so hard seeing him that way, despite knowing that his injuries would heal. At least, the physical ones would. She had no way of knowing what effect the attack might have had on him mentally. Was it the attack, or her betrayal of his trust, that had hardened him so?

Gone was the sweet, fun-loving man she'd come to know so well over the years. But she, of all people, knew what it was like to live with painful memories that were a struggle to keep at bay. Hers were of a childhood spent living on the streets with her momma. They were etched deep in her mind, but she'd learned how to hold them at bay, just as she prayed Jake would be able to do.

"Dinner was delicious, Mama Tully," Lila said as she placed her napkin on the table next to her plate.

Pulled from her troubled thoughts, Addy nodded. "You always did make the best buttermilk fried chicken." Not only had Mama Tully made that, she'd also baked some of her homemade scalloped potatoes to go with it. Addy had forgotten how good a homemade meal could be. Her own biological mother rarely cooked. And she herself spent most of her time creating pastries for the hotel or recipes for the cookbook she'd been working on in her spare time. Living alone as she did, she rarely cooked herself an actual meal with all the fixings like this one.

"It's so good to have family here to cook for," Mama Tully said, glancing around the dinner table.

Addy looked to Lila, returning her sister's misty-eyed smile. They were all still a family. Even after all the years they'd spent living apart from one another. Feeling emotion squeeze at her throat, she stood to help clear the dinner dishes from the table. She didn't do emotion well. Too many years spent hiding her feelings while growing up. According to the therapist she'd seen to work through some of her issues, it was also a big part of why she avoided romantic relationships. If you don't feel, you can't hurt.

Stepping away from the table, she carried the stack of plates she'd collected over to the sink. After placing them in the empty basin, she placed the stopper firmly into the sink drain, squirted some dish soap over them and turned on the faucet.

Mama Tully moved to stand beside her, easing the dirty silverware into the rising sudsy water. "It's so good having you home again," she said with a bright smile. "Maybe you can give me some pointers on making the perfect pecan pie while you're here."

"I'd be happy to."

"Gramma Landers cooks really good food, too," Finn said as he carried the half-empty pitcher of iced tea from the table to the refrigerator. "She makes the best peach cobbler."

"I remember," Addy replied as she turned to face him, her smile brought on by the memory of the time she'd spent with the Landerses, mainly Mrs. Landers, when she was a teenager, learning how to bake. "Your Gramma Landers taught me how to make all sorts of desserts when I was just a girl. I love peaches."

A tiny meow drifted out from under the

kitchen table, eliciting laughter from everyone in the room.

"Especially you, my little Peaches," Addy cooed. The cat sat peering up at her from beneath the fringed overhang of the tablecloth.

Grits and Honey, who had quickly accepted Addy's cat as one of their own, poked their heads out from either side of Peaches and barked almost simultaneously.

Mama Tully paused to look down at the two pairs of adoring eyes gazing up at her from beneath the table's edge. "My babies. Always so needy. Yes, you are loved bunches, too." She glanced up at the clock on the wall. "I should probably let you two out before the news comes on."

"Addy and I can finish up in here," Lila told her.

"I don't recall you ever making it a point to watch the news when I lived here," Addy said. Her foster mother had always preferred to spend her time after dinner sitting out on the porch or fussing with her vegetable garden rather than inside watching television.

"I realize this is a new side to me," Mama Tully explained. "But the days can be unbelievably long when you're lying in a hospital bed, unable to move about as you please. You read the Bible, make a few calls, do a crossword puzzle or two, study the subtle details of the pictures on the wall. But by the day's end, one becomes quite stir-crazy. So rather than count the peas on my plate when dinner was brought to my room, I chose to eat them while watching the news. It made me feel less out of touch with the world I live in."

Lila nodded in understanding. Addy thought about Jake, wondering if he had felt the same way when he was in the hospital after the attack. Especially being so far away from home. Or had he been in too much pain? She couldn't even begin to imagine what he'd gone through. To be shot in the shoulder was horrible enough, but then to suffer a broken leg on top of that was just unimaginable.

"The news," Mama Tully went on, a sheen of pooling tears filling her eyes, "serves to remind me of those days I spent in the hospital, and that, by the grace of God, I am alive today."

"Something we're so very grateful for," Lila said, stepping over to wrap her arms around their foster mother.

"So very grateful," Addy said. Joining them, she wrapped her arms around Mama Tully from the other side. No matter how hard it had been to return to Sweet Springs, she didn't regret being there. Not when it meant spending time with Mama Tully and Lila and Finn. The family of her heart.

Finn, not wanting to be left out, squeezed between his momma and Addy. "I love you, Gramma Tully."

"I love you, too, sweetie," she said with a sniffle. "All of you." Then she gasped. "Addy, the water!"

Addy followed her foster mother's gaze to see the dishwater close to overflowing, a thick layer of bubbles on the verge of spilling out over the front lip of the sink. Moving away from the embrace, she raced over to it. She turned off the tap and then attempted to scoop the escaping suds into the adjoining basin.

"Bubbles!" Finn exclaimed as he ran over to join her at the sink. Grinning excitedly, he dipped his hand in and cupped a handful of bubbles. Lila grabbed for several paper towels to wipe up the droplets falling from her son's hand onto the floor below.

"I'm so sorry," Addy said to Mama Tully. "I completely forgot I'd left the water running."

Her foster mother grinned, waving away Addy's worry. "I'm not worried about a little soapy water. We were having a moment."

Having a moment. Now that brought back some memories. Both she and Lila had experienced a few emotional roadblocks after coming to live with Mama Tully. That's how their foster mother had referred to those rough patches. The three usually got through them together, sometimes by coming together in a group hug. It was their way of reminding each other that they weren't alone; no matter what they were going through, they always had each other.

"No sense wasting all those suds," Lila said as she stepped over to swipe some of the shimmery bubbles from her son's upturned hand. Then she looked down at him with a grin as she smooshed the iridescent white blob onto the top of his head.

Finn ducked with a squeal. "Momma!"

Their playful antics brought a smile to Addy's face, a welcome reprieve from her troubled thoughts.

"Maybe you can just wash up in the sink tonight," Lila told him with a grin. "There certainly are enough soapy bubbles."

Mama Tully laughed. "We could give Honey and Grits their baths in there, too."

Honey, a corgi–Australian shepherd mix, barked as if in protest and then ran from the room.

Addy looked to Mama Tully. "I take it she doesn't like baths."

Her foster mother shook her head. "Not in the least."

Grits, however, wagged his nub of a tail excitedly.

"And he loves them," Lila said as she bent to scratch the full-blooded Australian shepherd behind his ear.

The pup barked excitedly, his mismatched eyes focused intently on Mama Tully.

"Uh-oh," Mama Tully said. "Looks like I'm going to be giving this eager little fellow a bath." She looked to Finn. "Would you mind giving me a hand?"

"Sure," he replied.

"This doesn't get you out of getting one yourself," Lila told him, humor lighting her eyes.

It was so good to see her friend so happy. She had always put on a smile for Finn over the years, but Addy knew Lila always carried the weight of her guilt around in her heart. Just as Addy had been forced to do with Jake as their friendship formed and grew.

"I know, Momma."

"Well," Mama Tully said, "let's go get Grits scrubbed before the news comes on." She looked to Addy and Lila. "Are you two okay seeing to the rest of the dishes?"

"Absolutely," Addy told her.

"Do you need any help?" Lila asked their foster mother.

"I think Finn and I can handle things. Come on, Grits. Let's go get you that bath."

Lila walked over to grab the remaining glasses from the kitchen table. "Are *you* okay?"

Addy stuffed the basket strainer back into the sink's drain to hold the remaining water in and then turned to face Lila. "Yes, why?"

"I know how hard seeing Jake was for you." Carrying the glasses over to where Addy stood at the sink, Lila set them down atop the counter. "But his wounds will heal."

Addy turned back around to start washing the dishes. "Not the wounds *I* caused him."

Lila glanced her way with a worried frown. "Addy, he forgave me. He'll forgive you, too."

"I'm not so sure he will," she told Lila. "Jake's so angry with me, and I can't say that I blame him for the way he feels. I broke his trust. Broke his entire family's trust, for that matter."

"Which you did for *me*," Lila said with a sigh as she reached for the nearby dish towel.

"But Jake found it in himself to forgive you," she said, hating the whine she heard in her voice as she voiced her thoughts aloud.

"I'm so sorry I brought you into the mess

I made of my life when I made the decision to run away from Sweet Springs."

"You were my best friend," Addy told her. "I wouldn't have wanted to be anywhere else but right there with you, supporting you in your 'messy life.'"

Lila sniffled softly.

Addy looked her way. "Please tell me you're not going to cry. It's all I can do as it is not to cry myself right now with my life the way it is." It was an admission she'd only make to someone she trusted. "And you know me— I'm not one to give in easily to the tears."

"Addy, I promise I'll talk to Jake for you. Mason will, too. We'll do whatever we can to turn his thoughts around where you're concerned. I know how close the two of you had gotten."

"It's not only my relationship with Jake that's pulling at me right now," she admitted.

"But Mama Tully's doing well," Lila assured her. "Truly she is. You don't need to worry about her."

Addy managed a small smile. "I know that. And for that I am so thankful. It's work that's adding to my worries."

"Why? What's going on?" Lila asked.

Since she'd been back to Sweet Springs, she and Lila had spent hours talking, about

Mama Tully, about her and Mason's wedding, and about Jake and how hard it had been for Addy to see him in that wheelchair. What she hadn't brought during any of her conversations with Mama Tully was her job situation. She felt bad enough that it had taken her so long to get there, thanks to all the upheaval she'd been dealing with at work.

Addy handed Lila the plate she'd just washed so she could dry it. "The Cozy Stay Inn was bought out. My job's been terminated."

"What?" Lila gasped. "But you've worked there forever. You're their head pastry chef and one of the most dedicated, hardworking people I know!"

Her friend's defense of her touched Addy's heart. "Mr. Mellott is having some serious health issues. The Van Helton Hotel chain has been trying to buy The Cozy Stay Inn for several years, so the time was finally right for him to sell it."

"Van Helton?" Lila said, eyes wide. "They're huge."

"They also like things done their way," Addy explained. "Which is why they are bringing in their own employees. Therefore, I will be looking for job openings online while I'm here." She couldn't bring herself to apply for work with the new chain. It just wouldn't be the same.

"Addy," Lila said with a sympathetic groan, "I'm so sorry."

She shrugged. "The good news is we all received a generous severance package. Enough to hold me over while I consider all my future career options."

"Mama Tully used to tell us that things happen in life for a reason," Lila said reflectively, offering Addy an empathetic smile. "And that new paths we find ourselves traveling on aren't really new paths at all. They're all still leading us in the same direction—to that of our future."

"I'm just trying to figure out where my path is taking me. At least where my job is concerned."

"You'll figure it out," Lila said determinedly. "And now that you're between jobs, you'll have more time to spend here with us."

"I'm probably going to be run out of this town the moment people find out I'm back."

"If Mason's family and the town can forgive me, they can certainly forgive you. Jake will, too. He just needs a little more time to get there because the two of you were so close."

"We *were*," she said sadly. "I miss what we had so much. You and Jake are my closest friends. Were," she said with a heavy sigh, "now that he's cut me out of his life. At least I still have you."

"Be patient with him, Addy. Jake's been through a lot."

"I know he has," Addy said, remembering all too well what it had felt like to see him in that wheelchair, his arm in a sling, leg in a cast. She sent up a silent prayer that her patience and determination would help her to save her unraveling friendship with Jake and bring with it his forgiveness of her. She just hoped God would be willing to take any prayers she cast up to Him under consideration. After all, she hadn't been to church since leaving Sweet Springs to go back to live with her biological momma all those years ago.

Addy's momma had never been strong in her faith, blaming God for all the years she'd spent struggling to survive on the streets with her young daughter. So they hadn't gone to church. Hadn't turned to the Lord for guidance. Therefore, she figured there was a good possibility that God and Jake were of like mind, not wanting to hear anything Addy had to say. But how could she change their opinions?

Jake sat in his wheelchair, staring out his bedroom window. His thoughts, for a change, were on something other than the tragedy that had befallen his group of missionaries. They were fixed on Adeline Mitchell. He'd hated Addy seeing him this way. Hated that she still had the ability to stir his heart when it had been dead for weeks. He didn't *want* to feel.

Thankfully, Addy seemed to have changed her mind about not giving up on him. She'd been back in Sweet Springs for nearly a week and he hadn't heard another peep from her. Not that he should have expected to. Addy had proven herself to be someone whose words lacked truth. As had Lila's before she'd come clean with his brother, he supposed. But he hadn't been in a relationship with her. Not that his and Addy's connection had been a romantic one. It had, however, meant something to him. The hurt her actions had caused him made forgiving her so much harder.

"Afternoon."

Jake cast a glance back over his shoulder to see his brother standing in the doorway.

Without waiting for a response, Mason stepped in through the open door. "I thought you might like to go for a—"

"Walk?" Jake finished for him with a grumble.

Mason's gaze lowered to the wheelchair and the casted leg Jake had elevated out in front of him. "I'll walk," he said with a shrug. "You'll roll."

"I'll pass," he muttered, returning his attention to the family's market across the way and the rows of trees behind it.

Sighing, Mason moved to stand beside Jake at the window, careful not to bump the extended leg rest. "Then we'll stay in your room and talk. It's been a while since we've spent any real time together."

He didn't want to exchange brotherly banter. It was too hard. He and Mason had always worked hard and laughed hard. At the present he wasn't capable of either.

"I was away," Jake stated. "And you've been busy building a house for you and Lila and Finn to live in after the wedding." Their father had left them all large parcels of land on the outskirts of the family orchards to build on once they were ready to start families of their own. Mason was more than ready at that point. Although he and Lila had postponed their wedding to give Jake time to heal. One more thing to add to the guilt he was already harboring. Guilt over his friend's death. Guilt over the worry he'd been causing his momma since his return home. Guilt over not being able to contribute to the family's workload.

"Well, you're home now," Mason replied. "And I'll never be too busy to spend time with my little brother."

"You need to focus on getting that house built." He frowned. "It's bad enough you and Lila felt the need to push your wedding back because of me."

"Of course we changed the date," Mason replied. "You're my brother. My other best man, besides Finn. We want you to enjoy being a part of our wedding day. Besides, Lila was relieved to have a little extra time to pull things together. It gives me more time to make the house I'm building for my family one they can truly think of as home. So it works out well for everyone in the end."

Jake nodded. "As long as you're not doing it solely for me." He motioned to his broken leg and the wheelchair he was seated in. "Because of *this*."

"We're not," his brother assured him. "Wedding aside, I'm worried about you."

"I'm fine."

"Jake, you're not fine," Mason argued, worry lines forming tiny creases above his dark brows. "You rarely leave this room. This conversation we're having is the most you've talked to any of us since you came home."

Jake turned his head to look up at him.

"Why would I want to leave my room? To do what, exactly? I can't work the orchards with you like I always have. I can't help Momma and Violet at the market. I can't even get around without someone pushing me because of this stupid bullet wound in my shoulder."

Mason sighed. "Your shoulder is mending. Your broken leg is going to heal, too. I know it's not easy living your life with physical limitations, but it's only temporary. Thank the Lord for that blessing. This could have been so much worse."

Like if he had died as well as Corey? "I realize that." He had thought of little else since returning home from his mission trip. No amount of his momma's suggestions that he should ask the Lord to help him through this made him reach for his Bible to read the passages he knew so well. Selections that had once given him comfort now had him questioning everything he'd been taught about his faith. About the Lord Who had not been there to guard His flock that day. Then Addy had shown up in Sweet Springs and pulled his troubled thoughts in her direction.

"I can't tell you how sorry I am that this happened to you," Mason said regretfully, his focus pinned on the cast. "If only I'd refused your offer to go on that mission trip in my place…" Emotion tightened his voice.

"Then you might have died that day," Jake said, knowing that only by the grace of God he himself hadn't. What he didn't understand was why the Lord had spared him yet had taken Corey. A devout Christian who was there to do work in the name of the Lord.

Mason's gaze snapped up to meet his.

"You had a son to think about," Jake explained, his tone softening. "And Lila. You made the right decision. Now stop worrying about me. I'll be fine. I just need some time to process everything."

"Jake, I know you," Mason said determinedly. "You're not processing. You're shutting down."

The response put Jake on the defensive. "I don't know what you're talking about."

"Momma, Violet and I all feel you pulling away." His brother's tone was filled with emotion. "Maybe you should consider talking to someone."

Jake tensed. "I don't need to talk to anyone. What I need is for everyone to give me some breathing room to sort things out on my own."

"If you're up to going to church…"

"I'm not," he said, the words clipped.

"Look, Mason, I'll get there. I know I will. I just need to do so in my own time. I'm asking you to respect that."

Mason shook his head and then held up his hands, palms out. "Okay. I'll back off for now. But know this, Jake, I will do whatever it takes to bring the brother I knew back to me. We're family, and family doesn't give up on each other—ever."

"Oh dear," Mama Tully said as she pulled a package of pork chops from the refrigerator.

Addy paused in setting the table and turned to face her foster mother. "Is something wrong?" After the rough summer Mama Tully had gone through after her emergency appendectomy and the complications that followed, Addy found herself worrying even when there was no need to.

"Only that my dinner is going to be ruined."

Her gaze dropped to the package in her foster mother's hand. "Did the pork chops go bad?"

"No, they're as fresh as they get," she replied, carrying them over to the counter by the sink. "It's dessert that's going to be ruined. I was going to make a peach trifle to go with our pork chops and gravy and completely forgot to run by this afternoon and pick up the peaches Constance set aside for me." She looked to Addy. "Would you be a dear and run over there and pick them up?"

"I…uh, sure," Addy said, anxious at the thought of heading over to the Landers place. Even if it was just to the market. Lila would have happily gone in her place, knowing the situation, but she and Finn were over at the new house.

Her foster mother let out a sigh of relief. "I'm so glad. A meal just isn't complete without dessert."

She'd be more than happy to go without, but she would do it for Mama Tully. "I'll be right back," Addy told her and then went to get her car keys.

Less than five minutes later, she was pulling into the market's parking lot. When she reached for the door, Addy found it locked. She leaned in to peek through the picture window, only to find the lights off. Stepping back, she glanced at the hours sign and frowned. The market had closed at four thirty. Her gaze shifted toward the house in the distance. Gathering up her courage, Addy crossed the yard and knocked on the door.

"Come on in!" someone inside responded. No, not someone—Jake.

Her heart gave an excited lurch, and then

anxiety washed over her. While she longed to see him, she knew Jake would not be happy to see her. She bit at her bottom lip and glanced back toward her car, debating whether to let herself into the house or go back to her car and drive away. If not for Mama Tully, she might have chosen to avoid the confrontation she knew awaited her inside. With a sigh, she let herself into the house.

"Jake," she called out as she stood in the entryway, "it's Addy."

There was a long stretch of silence before he responded. "I'm in here."

Following the sound of his voice, she stepped into the living room. Jake sat, his back mostly to her as he lounged in a tipped-back recliner. His wheelchair sat open next to him. At first glance, he appeared to be casually sitting. But he was anything but relaxed. Tension radiated from every inch of him. In the muscle clenched in his lightly whiskered jaw. In the rigid stillness of his shoulders. In the curl of his one hand into the cushioned arm of the chair. The other hand, protruding from the sling, was wrapped tightly around the remote. He had yet to look her way, not that she'd expected him to.

"Sorry to intrude," she said. "I was look-ing for your momma. I went by the market, but it was closed." Her gaze shifted to the old Western playing on the TV. Or, at least, that had been playing. The show had been paused. The scene frozen on the screen was that of a standoff in the middle of some fictitious town. It made her think of her relationship with Jake, only the standoff they were having was an emotional one instead of physical.

"She closed early today," Jake replied, his thumb now tapping the remote impatiently. "Lila wanted her to run by and see something they were doing with the new house."

"Oh," she said, frowning. "Mama Tully sent me over to pick up some peaches your momma set aside for her."

"That's why you're here?" he said, surprise easing his features.

"Yes."

"They're in the fridge," he said. "Momma told me *Mrs. Tully* would be stopping by to pick them up." He inclined his head in the direction of the kitchen. "You know where the fridge is. I'd get them for you, but…"

"Of course," she told him, needing no further explanation. "I'll just grab them and go so you can get back to your movie. I know how much you enjoy watching old Westerns."

"You, too," he said, much to her surprise. He hadn't forgotten her favorites. That meant so much when he was determined to give her so little. During Addy's last visit to Sweet Springs, they had sat through a cowboyathon, watching Old West-set shows together for practically an entire day.

"Yes," she said softly, "me, too." When he said nothing more, Addy said, "I'm sorry you had to go through what you did. If you ever need someone to talk to…"

"I don't," he muttered. "I told my brother the same thing earlier this afternoon."

"Okay," she replied, wishing they were back to how they'd once been. They'd been able to share so much. "Well, I had better get those peaches to Mama Tully. She needs them for the dessert she's making for dinner this evening."

Jake nodded and then turned his attention back to the television, hitting Play on the remote.

Addy wanted so badly to settle herself on the sofa next to the chair he was seated in and watch the rest of the movie with him. Wanted things between them to be the way they used to be. So comfortable and fun. Unfortunately, that wasn't going to change things.

Turning, she made her way to the kitchen. After grabbing the basket, she headed for the front door. As she passed by the entry to the living room, she slowed, taking in one final longing glance at Jake, who had gone back to watching his movie. Then she let herself out, easing the door shut behind her. Her heart, at that moment, felt as fragile and as empty as the tumbleweeds that blew about aimlessly in those beloved old Westerns.

Chapter Three

"I've really missed our family dinners," Addy said with a smile as she and Lila finished up that night's dishes. It had become a nightly ritual for them once again. A time to bond. A time to reflect. A time to forget her own troubles among the busy chatter that tended to fill the kitchen at every meal.

"Have you told Mama Tully about your job yet?" Lila asked as she placed several glasses into the cupboard by the refrigerator.

Addy shook her head, her gaze shifting to the kitchen doorway. "Not yet." After putting the leftovers away, Mama Tully had excused herself to go watch the news. Lila and Addy had taken to joining her once the dishes were done. It was amazing how much one could learn about the world in one brief hour. Addy didn't even own a television.

"She's going to find out sooner or later," Lila warned. "It's better she finds out what's going on from you. Believe me, I've been there, done that, and regretted not being honest with her from the start."

"I needed to know for myself that she was doing well," Addy explained. "Because if she seemed the least bit stressed about anything in her life, I wasn't about to add to it."

"She's good. Really, she is."

"I know." Addy nodded. "I'll talk to her tomorrow."

Lila smiled. "She's going to be so happy to know you're going to be sticking around longer than expected." Her smile sank slightly. "Not that she won't feel bad about you losing your job. None of us would have wished that on you."

Addy laughed. "It's okay. I knew what you meant. And to be honest, I'm glad to have this extra time to spend with everyone, especially you. Soon you'll be a married woman." One whose life would be filled with family moments and the love of a husband who adored her. Addy found herself wondering if she would ever find that same happiness. Shrugging the thought away, she added, "No more weekend visits where you and I throw on our pajamas and snack on popcorn while watching corny movies."

"Life does bring on changes, doesn't it?" Lila said reflectively. "But you will always be a part of our lives. I'll make sure to keep a supply of microwavable popcorn in the pantry for whenever you come to visit. I hope you know that you will always be welcome in our house, whether just for a visit or for a stay."

"I appreciate that. You'll just have to make certain Jake knows when those times will be so he can steer clear of me."

"By then there won't be a need for that," Lila said with such confidence that Addy almost believed her. "I have faith that everything will work out between the two of you. You just can't give up."

If only she had that same faith. She wanted to. Truly, she did. But it felt like she and Jake were so far away from each other now emotionally. Still, Lila was right. That would never change if Addy just sat around feeling sorry for herself during her stay there. Jake might have put up an emotional wall between them, but those walls could be taken down.

As soon as they were done with the supper dishes, Addy stepped out onto the porch and placed a hopeful call.

"Hello?"

"Hi," she said. "It's Addy."

"Well, this is a surprise," Mrs. Landers replied.

"If this is a bad time…"

"Not at all."

"I'm glad. I was hoping I might be able to talk to you about Jake," Addy told her. "I know he's been having a rough time of it."

"I've never seen him like this," Mrs. Landers replied with a heartbroken sigh. "He's still keeping to himself in his room. And when any of us go in there to visit with him, it's like pulling teeth to get him to talk. Even Mason, whom Jake has always been so close with, is getting nowhere."

"I'm so sorry to hear that," Addy said, her heart aching.

"The only spark I've seen in my son since he came home from his mission trip was the day you came by. You even managed to get him to come out of his room."

Only because he had wanted her out of his family's house. But she couldn't dwell on that. "I'm going to be staying in Sweet Springs longer than I had originally planned to, and I was wondering if I might be able to help you out with Jake."

"Help me?"

"I could come over for a few hours two or three times a week to sit with him." Addy winced at the desperation she heard in her own voice. But she wanted so badly to do this. To have this opportunity to right things. "I'm working on some new recipes for a cookbook I'm hoping to publish and thought I might be able to make some of them for Jake."

"They do say that a way to a man's heart, or, in this case, his good graces, is through his stomach," Mrs. Landers replied. "And I would greatly appreciate the chance to get caught up on stocking the shelves at The Perfect Peach. Things have fallen by the wayside recently. My focus has been on my son's recovery. Mason has been busy readying the orchards for winter and working on his and Lila's new house. And Violet, who is usually helping me at the peach market, has been filling in at The Flower Shack ever since Mrs. Benson had that stroke a couple of weeks ago. I told her Mrs. Benson needed her help more than I did."

Which Addy thought wasn't quite true, judging by the exhaustion she'd seen on Mrs. Landers's face when she'd last seen her. But her heart had always been giving, so it made sense that Jake's momma would be fully supportive of her daughter helping someone else in need. And Violet loved working with floral arrangements. She was the perfect person to cover for Mrs. Benson at The Flower Shack.

"Then you're okay with my coming over to the house to visit with Jake?"

"Yes, but you have to know that my son is not going to be as receptive to the idea as I am."

"I realize that," Addy admitted. "But I have to try. Jake's friendship is too important to me not to put the effort into repairing the damage that I've done. Besides, I've got thick skin," she assured his momma. "I can take whatever he has to dish out to me, knowing that it was my keeping the truth from him, from all of you, about Finn that left me in a bad place with him."

"Two wrongs don't make a right, Addy," Mrs. Landers said, her words tendered with kindness. "Life shouldn't be about paybacks. It should be about offering and receiving forgiveness."

She was so grateful that his family had chosen to look past what she had done, even if Jake hadn't. "I can't tell you how much it means to me. I'll do everything I can to help Jake through his recovery. Whether or not he'll choose to forgive me, only God knows. And He and I haven't really had a relationship since I left Mama Tully's to move back home with my momma."

"I see," Mrs. Landers said, but there was no judgment in her tone. "You never mentioned anything about that during any of our phone calls. I just assumed you had taken your newly found faith with you when you went back to Atlanta. You seemed so drawn into the Sunday sermons when you lived here."

"I was, but Momma blamed God for the troubles we had," Addy said honestly. Never once in the nearly four years Addy had lived with her momma and her new husband after returning to Atlanta had her family ever attended church services. "I felt like I had to choose between her and God after I left Sweet Springs."

"Of course you would choose your momma," Mrs. Landers said. "You were young, and I know how much you missed her when you were living here."

"I was happy with Mama Tully, but I did miss having Momma in my life," Addy admitted. "If the absence of faith in my life is going to be an issue for you, I'll understand if you'd rather not have my help with Jake."

"Honey, you were the only one able to get him to leave his room for any real length of time, to show emotion, to talk and even spend time outside on the porch." She let out a soft sniffle. "All those things I've not been able to do."

"He would have come around for you, too," Addy assured her.

"I'm not so sure. And faith can be lost just as it can be found again. That's something for you to decide. I'm not going to cast judgment on you because of it. I will, however, pray that you find God again someday. That being said, I would appreciate your help with my son more than you could ever know. In fact, you might just be the answer to my prayers."

A light tapping sounded, drawing Jake's gaze from the book he'd been trying to get his head into reading on his tablet to the closed door across the room. "It's unlocked," he called out. His gaze shifted to the clock on his nightstand, noting that his momma must have slept in for a change. He was glad for that. No matter how many times he'd told her he didn't need her waiting on him, she was always there a few minutes before eight, right before heading over to the market for a couple of hours, bringing him breakfast.

The door cracked open an inch or so. "Your breakfast is ready."

Jake's brows shot upward at the familiar voice. "Addy?"

"Yes," she replied through the slight opening.

She was the last person he expected to have knocking on his door, even if she had filled his thoughts since her return home more than a week ago. Especially at that time of the morning. He looked to the clock again for confirmation and then back to the multipaneled door. "It's 8:00 a.m."

"I know," she replied. "I'll give you a few minutes to get dressed before I wheel you out to eat."

"Wait a minute," he muttered. "Wheel me out?"

"To the kitchen," she clarified from the other side of the door. "To eat. Be back in a few." With that, she pulled the door closed.

"Addy!" he called out as her light footfall moved away.

She stopped somewhere in the hallway outside his room and replied calmly, "Yes?"

What on earth was going on? He wanted her gone, but that wouldn't get him the answers he sought.

"I'm already dressed," he told her. Had been for a while. Every day since returning home, he'd stirred to wakefulness long before the sun began stretching its dawning rays up into the morning sky. Then he'd dress and either sit in his wheelchair looking out the window or he'd prop himself up in bed and read a book. That morning, it had been the latter.

"Oh good," she said, sounding overly cheery as she stepped into the room. She was dressed in a pair of faded denim jeans and a burnt-orange sweater that made him think of turning leaves and pumpkins. "We won't need to reheat your waffles. So why don't you get in your chair?"

He blinked once. Twice. She was still there. Jake promptly lowered the tablet and shut his eyes, trying to determine if he had somehow fallen asleep while perusing the e-book and was only dreaming Addy's presence.

"Go away," Jake grumbled. "There's no place for you in my dreams."

"I could only be so lucky," she said, the humor clear in her voice.

Sighing, he opened his eyes once more to find her watching him with a grin. Forget it being a dream. He was caught up in a nightmare. Even if the center of that dream was a silvery-blue-eyed beauty. "Why are you here?"

"That seems to be your favorite question," Addy replied as she crossed the room to get his wheelchair. She pushed it up to the bed. "I'm here because breakfast is an important part of everyone's day. Now hop in and we'll see that you get yours."

He set his tablet aside and crossed his arms. He wasn't going anywhere, especially with her.

"Very well," she said, pushing the wheelchair aside so that she could move to stand next to the bed. "I'll bring your breakfast in here, and, because I promised your momma I would do this for her, I will see that you eat every single bite. Even if I have to feed them all to you myself."

He watched her go, took in that determined straightening of her spine and knew Addy meant what she said. "I'll eat in the kitchen," he called after her.

She stopped, taking a moment before turning around. It hadn't been long enough to suppress her entire triumphant grin. He'd caught the tail end of it before her expression turned impassive. "Good choice. And once you start feeling more energetic, you can help me fix us breakfast on the days I'm over here." Then Addy retrieved the wheelchair and wheeled it about so he could settle into it without much effort.

Jake fell silent as Addy pushed him out into

the hallway. The scent of bacon drifted out from the kitchen. He liked bacon, and Addy knew it. He snorted at the ridiculousness of it.

"Is something wrong?" she asked as they entered the kitchen.

He glanced back over his shoulder at her. "Did you really think you could win me over with bacon?"

She pushed him up to the table and set the brakes. "Actually, it's the maple-pecan waffles I made that I thought might do the trick. At the very least, help make you into the morning person you used to be."

Grumbling under his breath, Jake transferred himself into one of the kitchen chairs.

"Your momma's at the market, working on refilling the inventory. No doubt a little more at ease today because she knows her son is in good hands." She set a plate filled with bacon and her specialty waffles in front of him and then filled the two empty glasses on the table with orange juice.

"Addy, what's going on here?" he asked as she returned to join him at the table.

"I'm doing my best to make amends for the part I played in keeping Finn's existence a secret." Picking up a crisp piece of bacon, she bit into it. "Even if it means that my penance is going to be keeping you company several days a week and helping you get back to your old self. Because nothing's changed for me. I still care about you, Jake. I want you to get well and find your smile once more."

She cared about him? Her admission filled him with joy, but only for an instant. Addy couldn't truly have known what it meant to care about someone or she wouldn't have done what she'd done. "Several days a week?" he repeated, feeling his frown deepen.

She stabbed at a piece of syrup-drenched waffle. "Maybe longer," she answered with a shrug. "I guess that depends on how quickly your recovery progresses."

"I am definitely dreaming this," he decided. "Because there is no way this could be happening."

Addy glanced up at him from across the table. "Hard to dream when you're wide-awake," she said matter-of-factly. "But it's nice to know I can still have a place in your dreams. Now you'd best start eating before your breakfast gets cold. Of course, you can always warm it up in the microwave."

Lord help him. This woman was beyond persistent. With a sigh of what he was determined would only be temporary resignation, Jake sliced into one of the waffles. There was no sense letting a good meal go to waste. He would eat and then he would call Braden. If his best friend wasn't on duty at the fire station, there was a very good possibility he was lending a hand at The Flower Shack, helping Violet put floral arrangements together for Braden's grandma. Because that's what his friend and Mason did on their days off— help others. Jake had once been right there with them, making his contribution to those in need in their town. But now he was forced to sit, literally, on the sidelines and watch while others did what he yearned to do. Especially working out in the orchard. Thankfully, Braden had been stopping by to give Mason a hand with preparing the orchard for winter since Jake was currently incapable of doing so with his injuries.

"Would you like some coffee?" Addy asked, drawing Jake's attention back to what he was trying to avoid looking at—her far-too-pretty face. The woman he'd once dreamed about a future with. Not that anyone had known about those longings. Not even Mason or Braden. If only things were the way they used to be. To make matters worse, she smiled at him. "Your momma made some before leaving this morning. I'd be happy to pour you a cup."

"Thanks, but juice is enough." Jake stabbed

at one of the sectioned pieces he'd cut from his waffle and shoved it into his mouth. Maple syrup stirred his taste buds to life. Bits and pieces of what tasted like candied pecans and cinnamon filled every chew. And something else he couldn't quite put his finger on. Jake couldn't contain his groan.

Addy's face lit up. "Good?"

"Beyond good," he was forced to admit.

"Is there anything you would change about the waffles?" she asked eagerly. "Less cinnamon? More vanilla?"

"Vanilla?" he said, taking another bite. "That's the ingredient I couldn't quite pin down." It dawned on him that she was leaning forward, truly eager to hear his opinion. "I wouldn't change it. It's good the way it is." He glanced up, meeting her gaze. "Why does it matter what I think about your waffles?" She hadn't cared about his feelings when she'd kept the fact that he had a nephew from him.

"Because I'm working on a cookbook," she replied, easing back in her chair. "I've got to make sure the recipes are the best they can be before putting it out there among all the others."

He took another bite, savoring its sweetness. "I'd say you've got this recipe as perfect as it will ever be. But why try it out on me?"

She smiled. "Because I know you, of all people, would tell me if it wasn't good. Especially now that I'm far from being in your good graces. In fact, I'm hoping to try more out on you over the coming weeks."

His brow lifted. "So I'm to become your recipe guinea pig?" Why did his response have to sound so eager? He had no intention of letting Addy come back after this day, food or not. He just prayed it wouldn't be too long before his shoulder had healed enough to allow him to get around in his wheelchair without anyone's help. Most especially hers.

Addy smiled at him from across the table. "You love sweets and pastries more than anyone else I know. I can't think of anyone better to seek an opinion from when it comes to my recipes."

The front door opened and then closed, bringing an end to their conversation.

"Jake?" Mason called out a few moments later.

"In here," he answered.

When his brother stepped into the kitchen and took in the sight of Addy seated at the kitchen table, sharing breakfast with Jake, his eyes widened. "I'm sorry," he said, pausing in the doorway. "I didn't realize you had company."

"I don't," Jake said as he reached for his glass of juice, not wanting his brother to misread the situation.

Mason looked to Addy. "Morning."

"Morning," she replied with a smile. "I'm more your brother's jailer than his company."

Jake choked on the swallow of orange juice he'd just taken.

Addy flew out of her chair to stand at his side.

"I'm all right. Wrong pipe," he said, the words strained as he gasped for air.

Her hand came to rest on his back. "Are you sure you're okay?" she asked, slender brows creased in worry.

Jake fought the urge to give another sputter or two to keep her there. But his better senses prevailed over his foolish heart's yearnings. "I'm sure. Feel free to return to your breakfast."

She pulled her hand away, a slight flush filling her cheeks.

Mason sniffed the air around him. "I came in for some coffee, but something smells even better."

"I made waffles," Addy said, getting up from the table. "Would you like some?"

"I might have time for a waffle or two," his brother replied. "But you can sit right back down," he told her as he crossed the kitchen to grab a plate from the cupboard. "You're company."

Jake cleared his throat in disagreement.

Ignoring him, Mason said, "I'm perfectly capable of fixing my plate myself."

Jake felt Addy's gaze sweep in his direction as she settled down into her seat again, and his appetite slid away. He didn't want to have to depend on anyone to do anything for him. *Especially* Addy.

Mason, as if just realizing what he had said, looked to Jake apologetically. "I didn't mean to—"

"Forget about it," Jake said, keeping his emotions reined in. "It is what it is." But Lord willing, it wouldn't be that way for long. He missed spending his days out in the orchard working with his brother. Missed going on walks through the woods with his nephew. Finn was like a sponge, soaking up every bit of information Jake had to share with him. Things he would have shared with his nephew along the way if he'd been aware of the boy's existence.

"He'll be back on his own two feet before he knows it," Addy said, drawing Jake's focus back to the present.

Mason nodded, his gaze moving to Jake.

"I have no doubt. My brother is as stubborn as the day is long, so nothing's going to keep him down for long. Add that to the prayers he's got going up from the entire town, and recovery's going to be a cakewalk for him." He settled into the chair next to Jake and started cutting into one of the waffles he'd helped himself to. Then he paused. "Okay, I have to ask. How did *this* happen?" He gestured to Addy and then to Jake with his fork with a grin. "Addy becoming your 'jailer' and all."

"So you weren't a part of it?" Jake said in surprise, relieved to know his brother hadn't been an accomplice.

Confusion lit Mason's eyes. "I'm not even sure what 'this' is," he said, shoving a bite of waffle into his mouth.

"I offered to spend a few days a week with Jake while your momma catches up on some things she'd been neglecting at the market," Addy explained. "I told her I would help him out and make some food on those days. It gives me a chance to try out a few of the new recipes I came up with." She looked to Jake. "Although I'm not sure I'll be coming back again."

Was she? Jake was torn over that one. He'd

never thought he'd ever talk to Addy again after what she'd done, let alone share breakfast with her. But here he was. A part of him wanted to hold on to his anger toward her, because anger was far easier to deal with than hurt and guilt. Two emotions he'd been swallowed up by over the past few months. The other part of him knew that every bit as much as his momma had been thinking only of him, it was time for him to think of her. Despite his protestations, his momma had been wearing herself thin trying to care for him on top of everything.

"You might as well," Jake muttered, his response bringing about looks of surprise on both Addy and his brother's face. "I'm your best bet for a recipe tester," he explained, nodding toward the nearby wheelchair. "I can't run away."

The smile that moved across Addy's face with his reply hit him like that first ray of sunshine in the dawning sky. It was bright, soothing, with an unspoken promise of pushing any gathering storm clouds away. Lord knew he could use fewer storm clouds in his life. If it were anyone but Addy, he would welcome it without hesitation. But homemade waffles and pretty smiles couldn't repair the damage to their bond. She'd broken his trust. Smashed it to pieces. How did one ever get past something like that?

Chapter Four

Addy stood up from the porch chair and then turned to Jake with a smile. It was the third time she'd come over to spend time with him. So far, so good. "Would you like me to go get you another crepe?"

"Yes, I would," he replied, and then added with a slight frown, "but I'm going to pass on it. Hard to work the indulgences off when I have an arm in a sling and can't put any weight on my broken leg."

Jake had always been an outdoors kind of man, always into something physically demanding. He'd gone hiking, built things for both the market and while on mission trips, and lifted and carried filled peach crates to and fro. But to point that out would only serve as a reminder of all he couldn't do until he'd healed fully. So for now he would spend his time reading, researching upgrades for the orchard, and, when Addy was there, spend time out on the porch in what was more or less one-sided conversation. That was because he couldn't bring himself to open up to her like he used to. But Addy picked up the slack and chatted on about Mama Tully's dogs, wedding preparations for Lila and Mason's wedding, and other lighthearted subjects. While it made no sense at all, he'd almost begun to look forward to her visits.

"That will keep me from overindulging, too," Addy said as she reached for his empty plate. Stacking it atop her own, she said, "I'll go wash our dishes before the chocolate drizzle dries on the plate. Will you be all right out here?"

"I'll just stay where I am," Jake replied with that look of frustration he always got whenever she offered to do something for him.

She'd been back in Sweet Springs for just over two weeks, but it felt like so much longer. Maybe because she spent days just wanting her world to be right again. It had been five days since Jake had agreed to accept Addy into his life—temporarily. For a few hours on three of those days, she'd kept Jake company. While she might have been making better headway if they were together every day, Addy was grateful for any time she could get with him. Even if she was the one who did most of the talking whenever they were together. Being with Jake still felt good and fed her hope of repairing at least some of the damage she'd done to their friendship. When she'd lost her job she'd been devastated. But it had, in fact, been a blessing, giving her some much-needed time to devote to her personal life.

"Okay," she said with a nod before making her way back inside. As was their newly forming routine. On the days she came over, they would share breakfast she'd made for them. Then they would either sit out on the porch or move to the living room where they would spend a couple of hours watching television. At least Jake would. Her focus always drifted over to where he sat in the recliner chair, longing for the comradery they'd once shared. Then he would ask to be taken to his room so he could rest, and she would head back to Mama Tully's place.

Moments later, she stepped out onto the front porch to join Jake who, no doubt using his good leg, had maneuvered himself in his wheelchair over to the porch railing. He now sat gazing off into the orchard.

Addy was about to remind him that he was still healing, and that she would have been more than happy to push him across the porch, when she noted that he wasn't looking off into the distance anymore. Instead, his eyes were squeezed shut, head hung slightly. Had he hurt himself in his effort to prove he didn't need her help?

"Jake," she groaned in both frustration and empathy.

His head snapped up, his unbound arm coming up to swipe across his face with the back of his sleeve. "Stupid allergies."

Since when had Jake developed allergies? Addy's heart squeezed knowingly. It wasn't allergies affecting him. The sheen she'd seen in his eyes came from pain, probably physical and emotional, if she had to guess. But that was Jake, determined to keep his suffering to himself.

Sighing, she started toward him. "You might prefer to suffer in silence, but I'm not about to stand around and watch you do so. Let's get you inside and get some pain medicine in you to help ease your discomfort."

"No," he ground out, halting her steps.

"No? Jake don't be silly," she scolded lightly. "There's no reason for you to sit there hurting the way you are when your doctor prescribed you medication."

"I'm not hurting," he grumbled, averting his gaze. "Just dealing with a few things in my head. In fact, you might as well call it a day here. I'm sure you and Lila have plenty of wedding plans that need to be mulled over. I'm just going to sit out here and think."

"The doctor expects him to make a complete recovery physically." Lila's words from that day shoved their way into her thoughts. Did he actually think she could just *call it a day*?

"Lila and I can work on wedding plans this evening," she told him as she crossed over to where he sat. Lifting her hand, she let it hover over his shoulder for a long moment before lowering it. "I'm not going anywhere, Jake. Other than into the house if you'd like some time alone. If you feel like talking, I'm a good listener. Anything you need, just ask. I'm all yours for the afternoon."

All his. How many years had he longed to hear those words? Instead of soothing him, they twisted in his gut, right along with those already churning memories of the ambush. He turned his head to look up at her. "You want to know what I need, Addy? I need to go back to the life I used to live! I want to be able to go out into that orchard," he said, pointing toward the rows of peach trees, "and walk for miles. Or take the ATV up and down those rows, taking in the legacy my daddy left behind for us. Can you make that happen?"

Addy glanced toward the orchard.

"I'm sorry," he said with a frustrated sigh. "My inability to do those things isn't your doing."

Her gaze shifted back to Jake and then dropped down to his chair. He could see the wheels turning. Addy was a problem solver. Only some problems couldn't be solved. His injuries wouldn't heal any sooner just by her wishing it so.

"I can."

Jake's brows drew together in puzzlement. "Excuse me?"

"I can make it happen," she replied determinedly as she reached down to unlock the brakes on his wheelchair. Then she promptly stepped behind the chair and turned him toward the door.

"Addy, what are you doing?"

"Giving you what you need," she replied as she pushed him back inside. "An outing in the orchard." She guided him, broken leg extended, carefully through the house and into the kitchen.

He didn't have to ask to know where she was headed. Mason had built a temporary ramp off the back porch, making it easier to get Jake to any vehicle. Not that Jake had ventured out much. A doctor's appointment here. Physical therapy appointment there. And once out to see how Mason's new house was coming along. But pushing a grown man in a wheelchair across the softer ground of the backyard was no easy task. Definitely one he wanted to spare anyone having to do on his account.

"Addy…" he said as she opened the door leading to the back porch.

She paused to look his way.

"I appreciate what you're trying to do here, but—"

"But nothing," she countered stubbornly as she moved to turn his chair around, backing them both out onto the porch. "You need this, and I intend to give it to you."

"You don't understand," he argued. "It's not easy pushing this thing around in the grass. Especially with a man who's six feet tall, two hundred pounds, sitting in it. Even Mason has to put some effort into it."

"I'm stronger than I look," she told him as

she eased his chair down the ramp and onto the freshly mown grass. "I am a pastry chef, after all. That means I've stirred, or kneaded, countless bowls of batter and dough by hand many times over the years. A little bit of grass isn't going to stop me."

"Evidently not," he muttered with a shake of his head. Addy was determined if anything. And when she set her mind to something, she made it happen. He had always admired that in her. Admittedly, he still did. Jake's gaze drifted over to rest longingly on the tree line of the nearby orchard.

"Wheelchair or ATV?" she asked.

He craned his neck around to look up at her. "What?"

"To venture through the orchards in," she clarified. "Now choose one or the other or I'll do it for you. It's far too beautiful out this morning not to take advantage of the perfect weather."

A slight grin tugged at Jake's mouth. "Are you this bossy with everyone you know, or just those who are left at your mercy?"

She smiled. "Only when it's for the better of someone I care about. So what is it, Jake? Wheelchair or ATV?"

She wanted to take him around the orchard in the Gator? He chuckled. "Have you ever driven an ATV?" Those few times she'd come back to visit, he had been the one to drive them around. And he highly doubted she would have had much chance to drive an ATV around while living in Atlanta.

"No," she admitted. "But I'm a fast learner."

He grinned, feeling a bit of his lightheartedness return. "Now this I'd like to see."

"You're on," she said excitedly. Turning his chair, they headed for the pole barn where the mowers and ATVs had always been kept.

A few minutes later, they were seated in Jake's Gator. He and both of his siblings each used their ATVs to traverse the property and, in his and Mason's case, check on the orchards.

"You sure you want to do this?" he asked. "I mean, this isn't like running a hand mixer. We might both end up in a wheelchair."

"I'll have you know, a hand mixer takes a certain amount of skill to use properly. There are different speeds for a reason." She gave the front of the ATV a quick looking over. "Let's see. A steering wheel. A gearshift on the floor between the seats. A gas pedal and a brake. Looks doable."

"Ready when you are," he said, easing back in the seat, his casted leg stretched out in front of him.

"One sec," Addy replied as she leaned across him to grab for his seat belt. "Since I know you won't ask for help." She buckled him in and then sat back with a smile. "Safety first."

"I appreciate your taking such good care of me. Now let's see what you can do," he said with a nod.

She put the Gator into gear and eased it out of the building, Jake's wheelchair placed securely inside the rear cargo box in case they broke down or decided to get out for a bit somewhere along the way.

"This isn't Sunday," Jake muttered.

Addy looked his way. "Excuse me?"

"You're driving this thing like you're out for a leisurely Sunday drive," he told her with a grin. "In case you missed it, we were just passed by a three-legged turtle."

She arched a slender, dark brow. "A three-legged turtle?"

He gave a slight shrug. "It might have had four legs. It went by us too fast to really know for sure."

Addy let out a soft snort of laughter. "Well, we certainly can't have that happening again." As they turned onto one of the worn paths between a row of peach trees, she pressed down on the gas pedal, and the

ATV picked up speed. "Better?" she asked, glancing his way.

He chuckled. "Better." Thankfully, the ground between the rows of peach trees was mostly smooth, having been walked and driven on for more than fifty years. "Take a right up here," Jake instructed as they approached an intersection in the orchard. "I'd like to take a look at the newer crop we put in behind Mrs. Tully's place. It's part of our orchard's future."

"It looked to be thriving when I took a walk through it the other day," she told him. "Not that I'm an expert on peach trees. Peaches are a different story. When I worked for The Cozy Stay Inn, I would make all sorts of specialty pastries using them. Some were ones your momma taught me how to make."

Jake looked her way. "When?"

Addy looked Jake's way in confusion. "What?"

"You said *when* you worked for The Cozy Stay Inn," he pointed out. "I didn't realize you had left there. Momma never said anything about you going to work elsewhere."

Her smile fell away.

"Addy?" he pressed with a worried frown. She looked away, fixing her gaze on the wide dirt and grass path ahead. "The hotel was recently bought out. We were all let go."

"I'm sorry to hear that."

The apology sounded genuine, compassion she wasn't sure she deserved from him. She shrugged, trying not to let him see how deeply that had affected her. "I'm trying to look at the bright side," she told him. "It's freed me up to come back here to Sweet Springs and stay for much longer than I had originally intended to. I get to spend even more time with the people I care about, including helping Lila with any wedding plans she needs my help with. And, lastly, it'll give me a chance to really focus on the cookbook I'm working on. Maybe I'll even have it up for sale before Thanksgiving."

"You think it'll be ready to go that soon?" he asked. "Not that I know anything about publishing books."

"There's a good chance," she said with a nod, feeling that familiar surge of excitement that came whenever she thought about her project.

"I always thought publication was a lengthy process."

"It can be if you're going through traditional means. I'm not. I'll be self-publishing the book myself, which will allow me to put it up for sale as soon as I have it ready to go. The cover's already been created, and I've been taking pictures of the finished recipes to insert at the top of each recipe's page, just above the ingredient list and instructions inside the cookbook."

"Sounds like you've got things well under control," he acknowledged with a nod.

"I hope so," she said. "If the cookbook's a success, I intend to put a second one together. Which is why I'm still continuing to create and test new recipes."

"Will they both be dessert cookbooks?" he asked, sounding genuinely interested, much to Addy's surprise.

"This first one will be. Each dessert or pastry will be published with two recipe options. The first will be more simplified, for those on a tighter budget. The second will have a few added specialty ingredients for those wanting to be a little more adventurous with their recipe. The second cookbook I'm still debating on. Possibly an offering of dessert, appetizer and meal recipes." Addy caught herself and felt warmth fill her cheeks. "Sorry. I'm needlessly rambling on."

"No reason to apologize," he told her. "It's interesting. I've never known anyone who published, or even planned to publish, a book before. What made you decide to go it on your own?"

Recognizing where they were, Addy eased up on the gas. Another turn put them on the path that ran between the first and second row of peach trees behind Mama Tully's house. "I wanted more control over my cookbook content, its cover and the earnings it will hopefully bring in. I intend to donate a portion of the sales to an Atlanta-based charity I've contributed to in the past that helps single mothers who are going through hard times."

"A cause that touches close to home," he acknowledged.

"Yes," she said, unable to keep the emotion it stirred from her voice.

He glanced her way. "Things might not be where they once were between us, but I still wish you success with that endeavor."

"I appreciate that," she said, desperately missing their friendship. But she knew that forgiveness was something that couldn't be forced. If, and when, it came, it would be when Jake was ready. No sooner.

"Uncle Jake!"

Their gazes were drawn to Finn. He was making a beeline through Mama Tully's backyard. Grits and Honey were chasing after him, barking excitedly.

Addy brought the ATV to a stop and cut the engine. There was no missing the joy that spread across Jake's face at the sight of his nephew.

The dogs shot out around Finn, beating him to the vehicle. "Careful," Addy gasped as the pups jumped up at Jake, demanding his attention.

"They're fine," he assured her with a chuckle as he reached out to give each dog a quick scratch behind the ear.

"But your broken leg…"

"Is tucked safely away inside the Gator," he pointed out.

Finn moved to stand beside the all-terrain vehicle. "How come Aunt Addy is driving you around?"

"Because my right leg's in a cast," Jake explained. "Makes it a little hard to operate the gas pedal and brake."

"I could drive you around," Finn offered.

"I might have to take you up on that offer," Jake replied with a smile.

"What's your momma up to?" Addy asked.

"She ran into town to get Gramma Tully some things from the grocery store." He looked to Jake. "Will you be coming out of the house now? Momma said you would once you started feeling better. I've really missed you."

Jake winced, and Addy knew it wasn't from pain. "I've missed you, too. I have a feeling your aunt Addy will be getting me out more often," he said with a glance in her direction. "We'll make sure to stop by to see you when we're out and about."

"Really?" he asked in surprise.

Jake nodded his reply.

Addy understood Finn's surprise. Jake had pretty much shut himself off from everyone after coming home. Earlier on the porch, she'd worried that Jake might be getting pulled back into the emotional darkness he'd been in when he'd first come home. Lila had told Addy about it so that she would be mentally prepared when she began spending time with Jake. But during their outing that morning, it had been as if new life had been breathed into him.

Grits, not fond of standing still, barked with impatience. Honey followed suit and then attempted to wrest the rubber ball Finn was holding from his grasp.

"Hey!" Finn said as he raised his hand out of the smaller dog's reach. "You have to wait until I throw it."

Jake chuckled. "We'd best let you get back to playing ball with these two."

"But you just got here," his nephew whined.

"I know," Jake replied. "But I'll be seeing more of you now that I'm healing up."

"Promise?"

"Promise."

"Time to go," Addy told them. "We don't want your uncle Jake overdoing it today. I gave my word to your gramma Landers to take care of him while she's working at the market."

Finn backed away from the ATV as Addy started the engine.

"See you at dinner," she told him with a smile.

With a quick wave, he turned and raced off toward the house with the dogs.

Jake turned to find Addy smiling at him. "What?"

She put the ATV in gear and turned it around so they could make their way back. "You do realize that while you weren't stuck with me before, you are now."

Confusion knit his brows. "What do you mean?"

"Finn's going to be counting on me to get you out of the house and over to see him since you told him I would. So we'll be doing this again, because I have never, and will not ever, let that little boy down."

When her words were met with silence,

Addy glanced Jake's way. The smile he'd been sporting when they'd stopped to talk to Finn was gone. He was looking straight ahead, lips pressed firmly together.

Had their outing proven to be too much for him, and he'd sought to hide it behind a smile for Finn? "Jake? Are you in pain?"

"No."

She forced her focus back onto the path ahead when she'd rather it have been on Jake instead. Had stubbornness and pride kept him from telling her he was hurting? "If you've overdone things today, it's okay," she assured him. "You're going to get stronger with each passing day. We'll just take shorter rides for our next few outings."

No response.

Addy slowed the ATV and looked to Jake. "Can you please tell me what's wrong? I can't help you if I don't know."

He glanced her way, something akin to anger sparking in his eyes. "It's best if I don't say anything right now."

"If it's something I said or did…" she began, feeling confused by the sudden change in Jake's mood.

"All of the above," he said in a low growl. "You say there's no way you'd ever let Finn down, but isn't that exactly what you did keeping him from his daddy? From all of us?"

There was no denying the truth of his statement.

"I've tried, but I don't think I can ever get past that," Jake went on with a shake of his head, sparing her the need for a response to that accusatory question.

Her heart suddenly felt weighted down. Just when she'd allowed herself to have a sense of hope where her and Jake's friendship was concerned. That past week they had shared moments of teasing and laughter. Easy conversation. Smiles. And with just a few innocently spoken words, any of the headway she'd made with Jake was no more.

"I understand," Addy replied sadly. "But there's no changing the past. Even if I wanted to."

They drove the remainder of the way back to the house in uncomfortable silence. Jake settled himself into his wheelchair, and then Addy pushed him up the ramp to the back porch and into the house. Maybe they could talk things through.

She came to a stop in the kitchen. "Would you like something to drink?"

"I'm tired," he muttered. "I think I'll rest

for a few hours. No need for you to stick around. Or come back tomorrow."

She didn't have to hear him say the words *or at all*. She'd heard them loud and clear. Addy fought back tears. She would not cry. Doing so wouldn't change anything. That was a lesson she'd learned as a very young child. All she could do was respect Jake's feelings where she was concerned. "Of course. Let's get you to your room." Grasping the handles at the back of his chair, she wheeled him to his room.

"I can handle it from here," he said the moment his chair cleared the bedroom doorway.

He was sending her away—again. Addy nodded in understanding, her heart pinching slightly. But she wasn't going to give up. Jake had cracked the door open. Now it was up to her to open it all the way.

Releasing the handle grips, Addy stepped back into the hallway. "Goodbye, Jake." Without waiting for a reply, she pulled the door closed and walked away. She would let his momma know that she felt it was for the best if she stayed away from Jake for the time being. Possibly forever, if that's what it took for him to be happy.

Chapter Five

"I still can't decide on which cake knife and server set to order for our reception," Lila said with a troubled frown as she scrolled down the internet page.

"Why not?" Mama Tully asked as she sat putting the monogrammed address labels Lila had ordered onto the reply envelopes.

"None of them feel special," she replied with a sigh. "I'm not a rhinestone kind of girl. The camo-handled set doesn't quite go with the simple lace and pastels. I suppose I could go with one of the plain silver sets. It's not like I'll be using it again after we cut our cake."

"I thought you were supposed to use it to cut the top of your cake that you'll keep in the freezer until your one-year anniversary," Addy muttered as she wove some pale pink ribbon in and out of the openings around the edge of an antique white doily. "Not that I'm an expert."

Mama Tully stood and crossed the dining room to the old hutch she kept her good silverware in. She withdrew a couple of pieces and came back to the table. "I'm not sure if you'd be interested in using these, but they could be your something old."

Lila gasped. "These were yours? From your wedding?"

"Yes," Mama Tully replied with a wistful smile.

"They're beautiful," Addy said as she admired the set, noting the tiny, stemmed rosebud on the handle of each piece. Would she ever find herself making plans for her own wedding? Jake's handsome face shoved its way front and center in her mind, making Addy blink. Why did he always have to invade her thoughts? Especially this particular one. Jake didn't even want her friendship. He'd certainly never marry her.

"They are," Lila agreed, running her finger over the slightly raised flower. Then she lifted her gaze to Mama Tully, tears shimmering in her eyes. "I would be honored to use these to cut my wedding cake."

"And your anniversary cake," Addy said,

feeling her own throat constricting with emotion. To make matters worse, all this talk of wedding cakes and flowers and looking forward to all the special memories to come made Addy realize how empty her own life was. At least in the romantic sense. It had never been something she'd invested her time into. Her career, and, more importantly, doing whatever it took to remain financially stable, had been her number one priority. She'd gone on a few dinner dates over the years, but none that made her want to pursue a more serious relationship. None that had her dreaming of white picket fences and babies. Maybe she wasn't cut out for the whole happily-ever-after thing. Not like Lila was.

An image of Jake, smiling at her as they rode around the orchard in the ATV, pushed forward in her thoughts. And then came the memory of how that day had ended. She'd tried calling Jake, but he'd let both her calls go to voicemail, which he hadn't returned. No surprise there.

"Addy?" Lila said. "I was hoping that keeping you busy today with all this," her friend said, motioning to the projects they had been working on for her and Mason's big day, "might help to distract you from what happened between you and Jake yesterday."

"It did," Addy said with a nod, moisture suddenly blurring her vision. "A little."

"Oh, sweetie," Mama Tully said with an empathetic smile. Reaching out, she gave Addy's hand a gentle squeeze. "Storms blow in and storms blow out."

"And then the sun will shine again," Lila assured her with a tender smile.

Addy wished she had their faith. But storms could also leave a path of destruction behind. In her case, it had been a wide swath of emotional wreckage. "Not in this case," she replied with a sigh. She looked to Lila, seeing worry where there should have only been happiness written on her face. "I'm sorry my situation is putting such a damper on our afternoon. This is supposed to be a happy time for you."

"Addy, I'm going to be marrying the man I love this coming spring. Nothing could ever put a damper on my happiness. It's yours that I'm worried about. Your life is in turmoil because of me."

"You didn't fire me," Addy said lightly.

"I'm talking about your relationship with Jake. I've tried talking to him, reminding him that I made you keep your promise not to tell anyone about Finn."

Mama Tully nodded in agreement.

"I appreciate your trying to talk to Jake.

And don't worry about me. I'll figure it out," Addy assured them. "I always do." She glanced down at her watch, checking the time. The Perfect Peach would be closing in a couple of hours. She had hoped that Jake might have a change of heart, that he would finally return her calls, but it was clear that his mind was set. There could be no more putting things off. She had to tell his momma that she wouldn't be able to help her out with Jake any longer. "Would you mind if I stepped away for a little bit?" Addy asked Lila.

"Are you okay?"

"I've been better," she answered honestly. "I've been stalling giving Jake's momma a call, hoping he might… It doesn't matter what I had hoped. His mind is clearly made up, and I need to tell Mrs. Landers that I won't be coming by tomorrow to spend time with her son. Or any time after that, either. But it's something I think I need to do in person instead. I thought that if I went over now I might be able to catch her at The Perfect Peach before it closes."

Lila nodded.

Addy glanced around. "I hate to leave in the middle of everything."

"We don't mind, sweetie," Mama Tully said.

"I'm sure we'll still be knee-deep in wedding planning when you get back," Lila agreed.

"Thank you." Addy stood from the table.

"Send Constance my regards," Mama Tully said with a warm smile as Addy crossed the room.

"I will," she replied and, with a wave of farewell, left the room.

After walking over to the Landerses' place, hoping the fresh air and sunshine might do her some good, Addy felt her emotions still being pulled in every direction. She stepped from the orchard path and then turned to head toward the market, but then stopped. Something on the front porch of the old house drew her attention that way. There, seated in his wheelchair near the porch's edge, was Jake, watching her. Her heart gave a wild flutter at the sight of him, something that had been happening with more frequency, despite knowing his reaction would be far different than hers.

Their gazes met and locked, and Addy stood for several drawn-out seconds, wondering what to do. Did she walk over and say hello now that he had seen her there? Or should she simply wave and be on her way, giving him what he wanted? Her out of his life.

The choice was made for her when Mason stepped outside, oblivious to her presence, and said something to Jake. His brother pulled his gaze from hers and nodded in response to whatever Mason had said. Then he was gone, Mason pushing him into the house and beyond her sight.

Addy remained where she was, wishing she were inside with Jake, sharing laughter as they had during their oh-so-brief truce. "Oh, Jake," she moaned softly. There'd been something in that brief moment of connection they'd shared moments before that fanned those dying embers of hope in her heart.

Realizing how foolish she must look standing there gazing yearningly at Jake's house, Addy turned away. She didn't want people thinking she was pining away for Jake Landers, a man who now only tolerated her presence. As she crossed the yard to the peach market, she found herself wondering if those assumptions might be more right than she cared to admit. The store lights were still on. She could see them through the oversize windows. That meant either Mrs. Landers or Violet was still inside. Possibly both. Addy stepped up onto the low porch and reached for the door.

A short melody played overhead as she

stepped inside, signaling someone's arrival. In this case, Addy's.

"I'll be with you in just a moment," a warm, welcoming voice called out from the back of the market.

Mrs. Landers. Addy moved in that direction, working her way between shelves of peach butter and packaged soups. "No rush," she hollered back. "It's just Addy."

A second later, Jake's momma poked her head around a display of candles a short distance away. "Well, hello," she greeted. "Come on around. I was just picking up glass. I broke a candle."

Addy hurried around the display stand to help.

"Well, this is an unexpected surprise," Mrs. Landers said as she grabbed for a nearby broom and dustpan.

Addy carried the pieces she'd collected over to a garbage can and then walked back over to join Mrs. Landers. "I probably should have called first."

"Nonsense. Stop by anytime. You just missed Violet," she told Addy. "She had a couple of floral arrangements she had to deliver to the funeral home for Mrs. Benson." Attaching the empty dustpan to the handle of the broom, she placed it up against the can and the wall and then turned back around to face Addy.

Addy said regretfully, "I'm afraid my being here isn't as nice a visit as you think."

Mrs. Landers stopped what she was doing to look up at Addy. "Does this have something to do with my son?"

She nodded. "Jake asked me not to come back again."

"Oh no," the other woman said with a worried frown. "I thought things were going well between the two of you. Jake's been so much more like his old self. Except," she said contemplatively, "now that I think about it, he was a bit off today. I put it up to his being worn out from your big outing yesterday. I understand you two went for a ride in the ATV."

"We did. But we came across Finn when we were out," she explained. "Jake promised he'd be seeing more of Finn now that he was healing up and getting out of the house. I playfully told Jake he was stuck with me, because Finn was going to be counting on me to get Jake over to see him and I have never let that little boy down. It was a reminder to your son that I *had* let Finn down by keeping his family from him. He told me it was something he just couldn't get past."

"Nonsense," Mrs. Landers said. "I'll talk to my son."

"Please don't," Addy pleaded. "I don't want him to feel like I'm making his family side against him. All I can do now is respect Jake's wishes and stay out of his life. I'm so sorry to let you down. I know you were counting on my helping out with Jake."

"No, I'm the one who's sorry, honey," she said with a deepening frown. "I knew how close the two of you were and thought that maybe if… Well, let's just say I was a meddling momma who, no matter how unintentional, caused you undue hurt."

"And I'm so grateful you gave me the chance to mend things with Jake. Even if it didn't work out the way I'd hoped it would."

"You've persevered through the hardest of times," Mrs. Landers told her. "You'll get through this, too. Just stay strong, honey. In the meantime, I'll send a prayer Heavenward asking the Lord to help Jake find it in his heart to finally forgive you."

"I appreciate that. It's so hard."

"Sweetie, you and Lila were both young girls forced to make adult decisions neither of you were fully prepared for at the time. There is no changing the past. But you do have the ability to change the direction of your future.

Some days that might take a little extra patience. And others a good bit of prayer."

Addy's vision blurred with tears. "I should have pushed Lila harder to tell Mason about Finn. But I didn't want her to take off and try to make a go of things on her own, like my momma did. At least Momma and I had a car to live in. Lila left Sweet Springs with next to nothing."

Empathy shaped Mrs. Landers's features. "I had no idea you and your momma went through that."

"Very few people know about the life we lived," Addy admitted, preferring to keep it that way. She'd said more than she'd meant to, but it was important to her that Jake's momma understood more clearly why everything had happened the way it had.

"I can't even begin to imagine what that must have been like for you." Mrs. Landers shook her head.

"I had always thought of myself as strong. Unbreakable. But I finally realized I needed help to deal with my past, and Momma saw that I got it."

"Sweetie, everyone has their breaking point," Mrs. Landers said softly. "I reached mine about six months after Calvin died. I'd spent the first few months after losing him in a state of numbness. Then when feeling finally began to return, it washed over me in the form of fear, along with a good bit of anger at the Lord for taking my husband from me, from our family."

"How did you get past your anger with God? Momma still blames Him for the kind of life we lived during those early years."

Jake's momma stepped over to the candle display. "While I wanted to direct my anger at the Lord, deep down I knew that I should have been thanking Him for giving me so many wonderful years with Calvin. For giving him and me a family to carry on the love we shared." She turned away, busying herself with straightening several peach-scented candles. "I spent hours baring my soul to the good Lord, and to Reverend Hutchins, who had taken over at the church after Calvin's passing. It helped to talk to someone outside my family. It kept the conversation as I worked through things less emotionally driven. And it kept my grief from burdening my children. They were suffering enough as it was. So who am I to judge anyone for keeping secrets?"

"That's why you forgave me so easily," Addy said in understanding. If only she still had her faith to cling to. Then maybe getting through this heartache with Jake wouldn't be quite as hard. Nor would dealing with her past at those times when the memories reared their ugly heads.

"It was a part of it," Mrs. Landers admitted. "But the biggest reason I chose to forgive you was because of my faith."

Addy sighed, a deep sadness pulling at her. "I wish my momma had the same deep connection to her faith that you and your family have."

"It's a personal choice everyone has to make on their own," Mrs. Landers replied with a kind smile. "True faith can't be forced. Even Jake, who has always been so close to God, has taken a step back since coming home. But I have faith he'll find his way back and start attending church with us again soon."

She had no idea Jake had pulled away from his church. He'd always been so committed to it.

The market door opened, the melody playing overhead signaling the arrival of a customer, bringing an end to their conversation.

"Welcome to The Perfect Peach," Jake's momma called out as she and Addy made their way to the front of the store. "Are you looking for anything special?"

"A cookie," came a giggled reply.

"Finn?" Addy said as they rounded a six-foot-tall shelving unit that held homemade peach pies, already boxed and ready to go out the door.

"Hi, Aunt Addy! Hi, Gramma Landers!"

Addy looked past him to the closed door, watching for Lila. When the door remained closed, she asked, "Where's your momma?"

"She went to the house to find Daddy and say hello to Uncle Jake," Finn explained. "We're going over to the new house today to work. I get to help."

"Of course you do," Addy said. "Your daddy's a smart man. He knows where to find good help."

"Wanna come see Uncle Jake with me?" Finn asked, his question directed at Addy.

"Oh, I…uh…" She struggled to find an excuse that wouldn't have Finn asking questions, wishing she didn't have to. Wishing Jake welcomed time spent with her as much as she did him.

"I believe your aunt Addy was just on her way home to do some baking," Mrs. Landers spoke up, no doubt understanding Addy's dilemma.

"Chocolate peanut butter banana nut bread," Addy suddenly announced.

Finn's eyes widened. "I love peanut butter!"

"And chocolate," Mrs. Landers chimed in.

"And bananas," Addy added, laughing softly. "I'll be sure to have you sample it for me after dinner tonight. You can let me know if it's good enough to go in my cookbook or not."

Finn's head bobbed up and down. "I'll do it." If only Jake had the same amount of enthusiasm when it came to her cooking for him. When it came to her in any regard. She prayed that would change before she had to go back to Atlanta.

"I didn't mean to put an end to your solitude on the porch," Mason said apologetically, his gaze fixed on Jake. "I know you wanted some time out there alone."

"I changed my mind," Jake replied, accepting the glass Lila was handing him with an appreciative nod. The moment he'd seen Addy emerge from the orchard's tree line, his heart had thudded against his chest. Life suddenly surging through that achingly numb organ. Something it seemed to only do around her. Under different circumstances, he and Addy might have someday found themselves planning a life together, just as his brother was doing with Lila. All he'd had to do was convince her that her being older made no difference when it came to matters of the heart. That a long-distance relationship could work if both of the people involved wanted it to. That being Mason's younger brother didn't mean the boy she'd known hadn't grown up into a man who wanted a family of his own.

Although she'd been a fair distance away when he'd caught sight of her, he'd have known Addy anywhere. Not just by her height. Addy had always been on the tall side, probably somewhere near five feet nine inches if he had to venture a guess. It was more the strength in the way she carried herself that made her stand out in a crowd. Chin high, shoulders back, as if she were always on a mission to get something done. Then there was that beautiful, dark, shiny hair of hers. He'd liked it long, but the more modern, sophisticated cut suited her, too. It drew one's attention to those thickly lashed silvery-blue eyes.

"And a giant dinosaur chased me through the orchard the other day."

Blinking, Jake looked to Lila. "Excuse me?"

She giggled. "Actually, it was a squirrel. And I suppose I was the one doing the following, since it scampered right past me, heading down the path before finally cutting off and disappearing into the trees."

Jake blinked again, trying to recall how dinosaurs and squirrels had come into their conversation.

Mason chuckled. "Since you have the look of complete bewilderment on your face, I'll fill you in. Lila was telling you about the porch swing we found for our new house and how she can't wait to spend time on it, soaking up the quiet, comfortable solitude as you'd been outside doing." He glanced Lila's way. "Keep in mind the swing's a two-seater for a reason."

She smiled up at him. "I'm more than willing to share my solitude with you."

"I'm still lost," Jake pointed out.

"Sorry," Mason said with a grin. "I tend to get sidetracked whenever Lila's around. Anyway, she was telling you all about her swing, but it was clear you weren't hearing a word she was saying."

"Talking about dinosaurs always gets Finn's attention whenever he's distracted," she said. "I figured it was worth a shot."

"It worked," Jake admitted. "A porch swing sounds like a perfect addition to your new home. I apologize for zoning out on you. I promise it wasn't intentional."

Her smile softened. "I know it wasn't. We're just glad we're able to spend a little time with you before heading over to the new house today."

"Same here," Jake told her.

"Does that mean you'll be coming out of your room more often?" Mason asked before taking a drink of his sweet tea.

"I'm taking it day by day," Jake told him. He couldn't promise anything more. It was too hard facing the world outside, not only physically but with the knowledge that because of him Corey would never again watch the clouds roll across the sky, inhale the sweet spring air, and so many other things people simply took for granted. It was something he thought about often, especially during the quiet moments when he and Addy were sitting out on the porch.

"I think getting out of your room helps," Mason said. "In fact, the most relaxed I've seen you since you came home was when I joined you and Addy for breakfast the other morning."

Jake tensed at the mention of Addy and the morning they'd spent together. He remembered the fun and the calm before the emotional storm had blown in.

"Mason," Lila said in soft warning.

"It's all right, Lila," Jake told her. "It's the truth. I won't deny it. That morning felt like old times. But that's not where Addy and I are now, and I'll admit that I regret the way I ended things that day. But it doesn't change anything." Lila's reaction told Jake that she was aware of what had happened between him and Addy the day before. "Truth is, I'm not in a place right now in my life to focus on my issues with Addy. Not with…"

"I understand," Lila said with an empathetic smile. "I'll say a prayer for you. Maybe the Lord can help you to find your way back to a better place."

"Better yet," Mason said, "go to church with us this Sunday. Ask Him yourself."

Jake gave a determined head shake. "I'm not there yet."

Mason frowned. "Then we'll pray for you until you're ready to do so yourself."

"Thank you."

"Finn was so excited to see you out the other day," Lila said, her cheery tone cutting through the emotion that had settled over the room. "He tells us he offered to drive you around until your leg gets better," Mason added. At the mention of their son, his brother reached out to cover Lila's hand with his own, giving it an affectionate squeeze.

His brother and Lila were blessedly happy together. Even after what she'd done to him. To their family. But Jake couldn't sit there in judgment of his brother as he, too, had chosen to forgive Lila. He'd done so for Finn's sake. To spare his nephew the emotional pain of a family at odds. However, with each passing day, he and Lila were growing closer.

"He did," Jake confirmed with a nod. "And I might just have to take him up on his offer."

The front door swung open in the entryway, and Finn strode into the room in the same way Mason often did. *Like father, like son* had come into play so many times since Finn had come into their lives. Oh, how he longed to have a son of his own. Or a daughter. The thought had no sooner passed through his mind than the image of a smiling Addy took its place.

"I'm ready to build now," Finn announced, saving Jake from himself. His nephew's grin spread wide beneath what appeared to be a milk mustache. "Gramma gave me milk *and* cookies. And I get to be Aunt Addy's taster after dinner. She's making a new recipe and it's up to me to tell her if it's good or not."

Jake fought the downward pull of his mouth at hearing that he'd been replaced as Addy's recipe tester, which made no sense at all. He was the one who had told her not to come back.

"Lucky you," Lila said. "Your aunt Addy is a wonderful cook. Did she happen to say what she's going to be making?"

"Chocolate peanut butter banana nut bread!"

Jake's stomach gave an involuntary rumble. He really should be the one tasting Addy's recipes. But, no, he'd allowed his feelings to overtake him, resulting in his shutting her out of his life—again.

"Any chance I could get an invite to dinner tonight?" Mason asked Lila.

She laughed softly. "You're always welcome to join us. You don't need an invitation."

"I suppose we should get going," Mason said. "We don't want to be late for dinner."

"And for chocolate peanut butter banana nut bread with milk," Finn added.

"Speaking of milk," Lila said, rising from the sofa, "we need to go scrub your face before we drive over to the house."

Finn scrunched his brows. "I took a bath last night," he said, as if his momma needed reminding of it. "And I don't need help anymore washing my face. I'm almost ten."

"That you are," she agreed, her love for her son shining in her eyes. "But you might want to wash that strip of dried milk off your lip before we go."

Finn's tongue swept out to capture the remaining crumbs and swipe his lip clean. Then he smiled up at his momma.

"Nice try," she said, laughing softly. "But the dried milk is still there." Placing a hand at the small of his back, she guided him toward the kitchen. "You're too young for a mustache of any sort," she told him as they left the room. "Even if it's only milk."

As their voices faded away, Mason sat forward on the sofa, his grin disappearing. Resting his elbows on his thighs, he threaded his fingers together. "Jake, what happened with you and Addy?" His brows knit together in concern. "Like I said, you two seemed to be genuinely enjoying each other's company at breakfast that day. And she's been coming around."

"As a favor to Momma."

"I think there's more to it than that for Addy," Mason replied.

He met his brother's worried gaze. "How am I supposed to explain what's going on between Addy and me when I don't even understand it? One minute I'm angry with her. The next I'm feeling like I used to toward her when things were right between us. Then, once again, things come up that remind me I never really knew who Addy was and that I would be a fool to trust her again."

"Let me tell you something," his brother said. "I'd rather have risked being proven a fool where Lila was concerned than to never have taken the chance. If I hadn't, I would have lived the rest of my life without Lila in it and my heart empty."

"I'm glad it worked out for you and Lila," Jake said, meaning it wholeheartedly. "But you loved Lila. Had never stopped loving her."

"And you feel nothing for Addy?"

"What?" Jake said, taken aback by the question. No, he didn't. Not after what she'd done. Not anymore.

"I suggest you take a deeper look inside your heart where Addy is concerned," Mason told him. "Because her actions wouldn't have affected you so greatly if you didn't still harbor some sort of affection for her. You've heard the saying—love hurts."

Jake tensed. "I think I know my own heart." Which was the problem. His heart wanted to forgive Addy, but his stubborn head was determined to hold out. Love or not.

Finn bounced into the room, a bundle of joyous energy as usual. "We're ready to go!"

Lila followed him into the room. "Finn is anxious to try his hand at hammering nails today," she explained with a smile in Jake's direction.

"Do you wanna come with us?" Finn asked Jake. "You could watch me and Daddy build our house."

"I'll be helping, too," Lila said.

"That's right," Mason nodded. "We're doing this as a family."

Do I want to watch them? That innocent question served as a reminder of where he was at in his life. Sitting on the sidelines, watching everyone else live their lives. Jake fought against a surge of self-pity. As he did whenever that feeling came over him, he thought about Corey, and guilt swamped him. Corey hadn't been given the chance to live through his injuries. Jake had. And yet there he was, wallowing again over what he wasn't able to be doing short term. By the grace of God, he would heal up. He would pick peaches again. He would drive his ATV. And someday, he would hammer nails into a house of his own. The Lord had given him a second chance. Could he find it in himself to do the same for Addy?

Jake managed a smile for his nephew. "If

your momma and daddy don't mind me tagging along, I'll go along for the ride."

"You will!" Finn exclaimed.

"You will?" Mason said in surprise.

Jake nodded. "For a little while."

"I can run you back if you get tired," Lila offered. "I can't wait for you to see how much has been done on the house since you were there last."

"I'll call Momma and let her know you're heading out with us," Mason said, wasting no time in pulling out his cell phone to make that call. Jake had no intention of pulling out. He'd already given Finn his word.

"Finn, how about giving me a push to my room before we go?" Jake said. "I want to throw on a sweatshirt."

He didn't have to be asked twice. Finn hurried around to the back of Jake's wheelchair, grabbing a hold of the rubber handle grips.

Jake looked to his brother. "We won't be long."

Mason nodded.

Finn backed the wheelchair away from the coffee table and turned it toward the open doorway.

"Be careful," Lila called out. "Your uncle's still healing up."

"I know," Finn said as he pushed Jake from the room.

"Maybe I'll be able to help you build your house someday," his nephew said as he pushed Jake down the hallway to his room.

His house. An image of a smiling Addy seated on a wide set of porch steps in front of a cedar-sided ranch house rose up in his mind. The house he planned to build someday on the land his daddy had left him. The house he'd one day hoped to raise a family in. If only she didn't look so right sitting there.

Chapter Six

Addy slipped out onto the porch, hoping a fresh dose of evening air might help to soothe her troubled thoughts. She'd always been taken by the night sky one saw beyond the city lights, with its blanket of stars twinkling ever so brightly. Only tonight, there seemed to be no easing her worries over Jake. And her focus was drawn in the direction of the moonlit orchard rather than the stars above.

Jake had made it clear he didn't want her near him, and she had, no matter how hard it had been, respected his wishes. But it didn't feel right doing so. It was like she was quitting on him. They'd come so close to mending the rift between them, and now they were right back where they'd started when she'd first come home.

Maybe this was where she needed to bare

her soul to the Lord, like Jake's momma had when she'd gone through a troubled time. But to do so, Addy knew she had to put her fear of God rejecting her aside and cling to what she'd once been taught of the Lord. He was merciful. He was forgiving. He was compassionate. He would lead her in the direction she was meant to go, and she would trust in His plans for her. Whatever they might be.

"I do trust in You," she said as she sat at the porch's edge, looking up into the twinkling heavens above.

"Addy?"

The screen door eased open behind her. Addy glanced back as Lila stepped out onto the porch. "Hi," she said with a forced smile.

Lila glanced around. "I thought I heard voices."

"Only me," Addy told her. "I was having a heart-to-heart with God."

"You were?"

Addy shrugged. "I figured it's as good a time as any to test the waters."

"Mind if I join you? I promise to sit here quietly."

"I think I've said all I have to say to God tonight," Addy said, motioning to the vacant area beside her.

"Couldn't sleep?" Lila asked as her gaze lifted to the sky.

"Not really. You?"

"Same. My mind's too full of wedding plans and house-decorating decisions." She looked to Addy. "Everything okay?"

"I feel like I'm always letting someone down," she said, hating the catch she heard in her voice as she spoke.

Lila leaned in and wrapped a supportive arm around her shoulders. "You've never let me down. Ever."

"And I never will," Addy said determinedly. "You are my dearest friend and the sister of my heart."

"As you are mine," Lila replied, a sheen of tears filling her eyes. "And I hate seeing you so unhappy. I wish things had worked out with you spending time with Jake."

"Me, too," Addy said, pasting on a smile as she fought to collect herself. "It was definitely the shortest job I've ever held." Humor had gotten her through the hard times in her life. Through the fear. Through the hunger. Through the separation from her momma. She prayed it might, if only in a small way, now ease some of the pain she felt over the loss of a friendship she'd held dear for so very long. Of the man she had come to care for far too deeply.

Lila offered an empathetic smile. "I'd say it lasted longer than either of us expected it would when Mrs. Landers accepted your offer to help out with Jake. To be honest, after his not-so-warm reception that first day, I was surprised he didn't send you packing the moment you showed up at his house that morning with your sunny smile and pecan waffles."

Still pondering her last thought, Addy nodded distractedly. "I suppose you're right. I was fortunate to have gotten to spend any time with him." She looked to Lila. "Those few days we spent together felt like everything was finally falling back into place for us. Like we'd once been with each other, at ease, sharing laughter over the silliest of things. I've missed that so much. Missed him so much," she added with a sigh.

"It's hard when someone you love shuts you out of their heart," Lila acknowledged with a nod. "I went through that with Mason, and it hurts so deeply."

Addy looked to Lila in confusion. "I don't love Jake." But the words, after she'd spoken them, rang far from true. How had that happened? When had her feelings gone from friendship to love?

"If that's what you've been telling yourself, then I think you need to look a little deeper into your heart," Lila replied. "I've been there during some of your calls to his momma, not that they knew I was there with you, and saw the way you reacted when Jake would commandeer the house phone before his momma could get to it. I saw the smiles that lit up your face. The joy that filled your voice. You can't tell me you don't feel something for Jake."

"Lila," Addy said, "Jake is…well, he's like a brother to me."

Lila raised a challenging brow.

"He's twenty-six," she said with a troubled frown. "I'm twenty-nine."

"Jake will be twenty-seven in January," her friend pointed out. "That's not even three years' difference between the two of you."

"But I'm older," she said, trying to make her friend see reason. But age was no longer an issue. She and Jake were both grown adults.

"So you're a cougar," Lila said with a shrug, followed by a grin.

Addy gave her a sisterly shove. "I am not a cougar."

Lila meowed aloud and pretended to swipe a claw.

"Momma?" Finn's voice sounded from the other side of the screen door.

Addy and Lila turned as the screen door creaked open and he stepped outside to join them.

"Honey, what are you doing up?" Lila asked. "Are you feeling okay?"

"I got up to get a drink of water and heard people talking out on the porch. Then I heard you meow."

Addy muffled a snort of laughter as she scooted away from Lila to make room for Finn to join them. "Have a seat," she offered, patting the porch floor beside her.

He settled himself down and looked up at his momma. "Why were you pretending to be a cat?"

"I…" she began, "well, your aunt Addy and I were…"

"Playing Name That Animal," Addy said, wondering if the Lord forgave little mistruths. Finn was too young to understand the workings of the heart. Or the depth of gratitude Addy felt toward Lila for lightening her mood when she was so confused over her feelings for Jake.

"Can I play?" he asked excitedly.

"Sure," Lila answered with a smile as she reached out to smooth down some of the sleep-mussed strands of his hair. "And it's your turn."

Finn pursed his lips, moving them up and down over and over again. He looked from Lila to Addy expectantly.

"You got anything?" Addy asked Lila.

"A baby bird?" she guessed.

"Nope," Finn said, shaking his head.

"We need a sound," Addy told him.

"Can't," Finn said, shaking his head. "I'd need a glass of water."

"Water?" She met Lila's equally confused gaze.

Finn erupted into laughter. "I'm a fish!"

Addy broke into laughter, too. Wrapping her arm around him, she gave him an affectionate squeeze.

"You win," Lila announced with a grin.

No, it was Addy who had won. Because she had these two very special people in her life. They, along with Mama Tully, would help get her through this heartache with Jake. Because no matter how deeply she felt for him, she had to accept that those feelings would never be reciprocated. You can't love someone you don't trust.

Chapter Seven

"Back to hiding away in your room all day?"

Jake's finger went to the power button on his tablet, shutting off the screen. "If you're looking for a sibling to annoy," he said, glaring at his brother from where he sat by the window, "I think Violet's over at the market with Momma."

Mason chuckled. "Actually, it's you I came to annoy." He crossed the room and sank down on the edge of Jake's bed. "What are you doing?" he asked earnestly.

Jake lowered his tablet to his lap facedown. "Just skimming the internet," he replied with a frown, grateful for his brother's untimely intervention. "Nothing better to do." The last thing he needed to be doing was searching for cookbooks. Especially when he was trying his best to avoid thinking about Addy.

Yet, there he'd been, perusing an online bookstore's cookbook section, thinking about how someday Addy's might be on there, too. He wouldn't even be able to congratulate her on her accomplishment because he'd shut her out of his life. Of his heart.

"Well, put that thing away," Mason told him. "We're taking a ride."

Jake looked at Mason questioningly.

Mason stepped forward to remove the tablet from Jake's lap and set it on the nearby nightstand. Only he placed it face up and froze, his gaze fixed on the screen.

"Like I said," Jake muttered, using his good arm to move his wheelchair, "nothing better to do."

His brother merely nodded in response, yet there were unspoken words in the stare Mason turned on him.

"Where are we taking a ride to?" Jake asked, trying to defuse the momentary discomfort of the situation.

"The house," his brother replied. "We just finished framing it in and Lila is, well, to say excited is putting it mildly. She wanted me to come get you and bring you over there to see it, so here I am."

"I was just out there."

"The house is changing every day."

"How about I wait until it's all done?" Jake suggested, not wanting to subject his soon-to-be sister-in-law to the dismal attitude he couldn't seem to shake. "I'm not really in the mood for an outing."

Mason pulled his cell phone from his jeans pocket and held it out to Jake. "Okay. Then how about you call and tell Lila you won't be coming?"

"Me?"

"In case you've forgotten, I've pledged my love to that woman," Mason explained. "That means I will do everything in my power to make her happy and to never let her down. And so here I stand." He gave the phone a shake. "You can do the letting down, not me. Oh, and just so you know, Finn is waiting to show you his new house's progress, too."

"As if the Lila thing wasn't guilt-inducing enough," Jake said with a sigh. "You have to go and toss the nephew card out onto the table."

Mason grinned. "Did it work?"

Ten minutes later, they were pulling up to the build site for his brother and Lila's new home. Jake took it all in, which he really hadn't done on his previous trips there. Mason had worked hard to create the perfect setting for the house he was building. He'd cleared away a few trees and leveled out the land around it, giving the home site a much cleaner line and appearance. In the center of the recently upturned and smoothed-out land arose a two-story structure. The plywood and wrap had been put on the outside, sealing up the framing that had been done when he'd last seen it, making it easy to visualize what the house would someday look like. A large cutout had been made in the front living room wall, where an oversize picture window would go. Lila had wanted it to be big, calling it her Christmas tree window.

Jake found his thoughts drifting to Addy. Did her dream house feature a grand window for displaying a Christmas tree, too? A large front porch with railing to wrap garland around? And lots of windows to hang wreaths on? Children? Because it was the kind of future he could see himself living—with her.

"Let's go check it out," Mason said, drawing Jake from his mind's wanderings.

Jake opened the passenger door and waited as Mason brought his wheelchair around to him. "I've got it," he said when Mason offered to help him down. He could do this. Needed to do it himself if he were ever going to get his life back to the way it had once been.

"I've put plywood down atop the walkway

to the house until it's ready to be poured," Mason told him as he pushed Jake toward the section of earth that had been carved out for their front sidewalk. "Lila thought it would make it easier for you to get to the house in your wheelchair or on crutches than pushing you through the gravel or dirt like we did last trip."

"That was kind of her," Jake said with a grateful nod. Then he noticed the ramp that had been constructed along the front of the porch at an angle. "You put in a ramp?" he said, a slight hitch to his voice as he took in all that his brother and Lila had done to enable him to see the progress they were making on their new home firsthand.

"Can't have you sitting outside looking in anymore when all the good stuff to see is inside," Mason told him as he maneuvered Jake's chair around to face the sidewalk's entrance. With a slight nudge, his brother had them moving up the makeshift walkway.

Lila stepped outside, a smile lighting her face. "Jake!" she called out with a welcoming wave.

"Uncle Jake!" Finn cried out as he shot out around his mother and down the ramp.

No matter how gloomy his day might seem, just the sight of his nephew always put a smile on Jake's face. "Looks like you've been working hard today," he told Finn as he walked alongside Jake's chair as Mason pushed him up to the porch.

"Uncle Braden's been helping, too," Finn explained as he raced up the ramp ahead of Mason and Jake.

Jake glanced off to the side where Braden's SUV was parked. He hadn't noticed it when they'd pulled up, but then, his focus had been on the setting for Mason's newly framed house. It didn't surprise him in the least that his best friend was there lending a hand. Braden had always been like a brother to them both. Even Finn thought of him as family now, which had led to him calling him Uncle Braden without the least bit of prompting.

Mason had just pushed Jake up the temporary ramp and onto the porch when Braden emerged from the house through the framed but doorless front entry. The second his gaze landed on Jake, a wide grin spread across his face. "Well, I'll be." He looked to Mason. "How did you manage to get this stubborn mule out here?"

"He made it about Lila and Finn," Jake answered for his brother. "There was no way I could let them down. They wanted me here to see the progress they've made on their house.

So here I am." And it felt good to be there, seeing his brother's excitement, Lila's, and especially his nephew's, over the building of their family's soon-to-be home.

Lila smiled. "And we're so glad you are." She looked to Mason. "Bring him in so he can see the rooms."

"Mine's in the back of the house," Finn said, bouncing around the porch like a human pogo stick. "I'll be able to see deer from my window when they come out of the woods."

"The perks of being the firstborn," Jake teased. "All I can see from my bedroom is the family market."

"I'll be out of the house soon," Mason reminded him. "My room's all yours if you want it." He eased the chair into the house, careful not to bump Jake's extended leg.

"Maybe after my leg heals, I'll consider switching," he replied. "My room's closer to the front door and kitchen. Less pushing for whoever gets stuck with wheelchair duty."

"It's not a duty," Mason said, all jesting leaving his voice. "You were injured while serving the Lord in my place. I would push you around for the rest of your life if you had required it. Even if you'd been injured in some other way, for that matter."

Jake knew his brother's words to be true.

"I know you would. I would do the same for you." Wanting to lighten up the moment, he added, "Guess I should feel blessed to have a brother who has a little bit of upper-body strength."

"Little bit?" Mason grumbled behind him.

"Don't go fishing for compliments from me," Jake said, biting back a grin. "That's Lila's job."

Braden snorted behind him. "Oh, the joys I missed being an only child."

"You and me both," Lila said with an exaggerated shake of her head.

They moved through the framed ranch-style house, Finn leading the tour. Jake found himself grateful that Mason had gotten him out of the house. It was a welcome distraction.

"This is my window," Finn announced when they entered what would be his new bedroom. Then he gasped, racing over to the hole where the window would soon go. "A deer!" he cried out, pointing outside.

Mason gave a chuckle as he moved to stand behind his son and peer out. "There sure is."

Lila stepped over to join them. "Oh, how adorable!"

"Guess we'd better go check out all the cuteness to be had in your brother's backyard," Braden said as he and Jake exchanged grins. Then he stepped around Jake's wheel-chair and pushed him over to where Lila and Mason stood with Finn.

They were so absorbed in watching the deer, none of them heard anyone pull up to the house. It wasn't until a "Hello?" carried back to the room they were gathered in that they knew someone had just come up onto the front porch.

"Lila?" another voice joined in.

Jake's thoughts froze and then went into a twisting jumble at the far-too-familiar sound of Addy's soft, lilting voice. His heart leapt with the anticipation of seeing her again, yet he felt woefully unprepared for it. He'd only just discovered the depth of his feelings for her. Was still trying to sort things out. He didn't know what to say. He glanced up at his brother accusingly.

Mason shrugged. "This wasn't planned. I swear," he said, keeping his voice low.

"We're back here," Lila called out. "In Finn's room."

Even with his back turned to them, Jake could hear his sister and Addy moving toward them through the house. It had been four days since what had started out as a surprisingly great day had ended up going all wrong. He'd sent her away but hadn't been able to push her from his thoughts, no matter how hard he'd tried. And now here she was. And here he was. If he weren't confined to a wheelchair, he might have actually considered making a quick exit through the open window hole.

"Well, hello," Lila greeted. "Did you come to see the progress we've made so far?"

"Momma sent us over with a picnic lunch," his sister said cheerily. "We left the basket out on the porch. But the house looks gr—Jake?" she half squeaked behind him. No doubt just realizing he was there across the room. The wheelchair alone was an immediate giveaway.

"Hey, Vi," he replied without glancing back. If he did, he knew his gaze would search Addy out no matter how many times he'd told himself he never wanted to see her again.

His plan to implement the out of sight, out of mind tactic went by the wayside as Braden turned Jake's chair around so that he was facing the group gathered in the room around him. Sure enough, he looked past his sister to where Addy stood. Apparently, she was as surprised to see him there as he was to see her. He sat, drinking in the sight of her even as he was telling himself to look away.

"What are you doing here?" Violet asked, thankfully forcing his gaze away from Addy and back to her. "Not that I'm not beyond thrilled to see you out and about," she promptly added.

"Daddy brought him," Finn answered for him. "I'm showing Uncle Jake my room."

"I wish I'd known you were over here," his sister said with a frown. "We're short a sandwich." Then she brightened. "But we have plenty of cookies. You could just fill up on those."

"Cookies!" Finn exclaimed and raced from the room.

"Save some for the rest of us!" Lila called after him.

"Jake can have my sandwich," Braden offered. "I've got to get going, anyway. I promised to look in on Granny this afternoon. I will, however, grab myself a cookie on the way out."

"But you've been here working all morning," Violet said with a troubled frown.

"You know Granny," Braden told her. "I won't be there five whole minutes before she'll be trying to stuff me like a Thanksgiving turkey with her cooking."

"Thanks for all your help today," Mason said.

"Yes," Lila agreed. "Thank you."

"Anytime."

"Give your granny my regards," Violet called after him.

"I will," he replied. "Oh, and I start my shift at the station tomorrow, or I'd offer to come by and help you at the flower shop."

"I'll be fine," she assured him.

"No doubt," he replied with a smile, and then, after saying his goodbyes, strode from the room.

Lila turned to Addy. "I'm so glad you came with Violet. What do you think? The house is really coming along, isn't it?"

"I think it's going to be wonderful," Addy replied, her gaze drifting back to Jake.

The regret he saw in those blue-gray eyes prodded at his heart. Jake looked away, struggling to keep that emotional wall up between them.

"Well, I guess I'll see you at home tonight," Addy said to Lila, her words sounding a little tight. "Would you mind bringing Mama Tully's picnic basket home with you when you come?"

"You're leaving already?" Lila said with a frown. "But you and Violet just got here."

"I was in the middle of edits on my cook-book when Violet called and asked if she could borrow Mama Tully's picnic basket," Addy explained.

"I asked Addy if she'd like to ride over here with me to drop off the sandwiches and cookies Momma made for you all and see how things were coming along with the house," Violet said. "I did promise her we wouldn't be gone long."

"I know how much that cookbook means to you," Lila said to Addy. "You go do what you need to do. You can come out another time when you can stay longer."

"Thank you for understanding," Addy replied with a grateful smile. "I really do want to have this cookbook up for sale by the time the holiday shopping madness begins."

"I'll walk you out," Lila told her. "I need to make sure my son doesn't eat more than his share of the cookies."

"I'll be right out," Violet told the two women. As soon as they had gone, his sister swung around, hands on her hips as she glared at Jake. "See what you did!"

"What did I do?" Jake asked in confusion.

"You made Addy feel unwelcome here."

Jake felt the remorse deep in his gut. "I didn't even say anything." Because he'd been so focused on not letting his feelings for Addy show, he'd unintentionally hurt hers.

"Exactly!" his sister snapped with a disapproving glare. Then she turned in a huff and left the room.

Jake watched her go through the open framing that made up the house's interior. He looked to Mason to see if he could make sense of their sister's accusation, only to find his brother scowling, too.

Jake groaned. "Not you, too."

"Would it have killed you to at least say hello to Addy?" his brother grumbled.

"I would have, but the girls were talking and then Violet and Braden started chattering on about his granny and the flower shop."

"Tell me something, little brother," Mason said. "How is it you can so easily forgive Lila for what she did, but not Addy?"

"Lila wasn't in constant contact with our family nearly every single week for years," Jake ground out, not appreciating being made to feel like he had done something wrong. "Addy had so many opportunities to reveal the truth to us, but she chose not to. How do I get past that?"

"You find a way. And keep in mind she'd given her word to Lila," Mason reminded him. "Her foster sister and best friend."

"You make it sound so simple."

"Life is never simple," his brother replied. "Nor is it perfect. Addy was wrong in what she did. Just as Lila was wrong. There's no denying our lives would have been far different if Lila hadn't run off and if Addy hadn't kept the truth from us. But it is what it is. I love Lila and was willing to forgive her for the hurt she caused me. Because that's the kind of man Daddy raised me to be."

Had raised them both to be, Jake acknowledged in silent pondering. Releasing a sigh of frustration, he said, "I don't know how to get there." He met Mason's gaze. "But I want to."

A slight smile pulled at his brother's lips. "Glad to hear it. I'd say the first step is finding a way to set your anger aside. Just like you did with Lila."

Jake nodded in agreement.

"I know you haven't felt up to going to church since coming home from your mission trip, but that doesn't mean you can't turn to the Lord for guidance," Mason said. "Ask Him to help you find the inner fortitude to forgive Addy. Be the kind of Christian our momma and daddy raised us to be."

Jake looked up at him. "I think you missed your calling, big brother. You've got so much of Daddy's goodness in you. You really would have made a fine preacher." If only he could get back to the man he'd been before his last mission trip. The tragedy he'd survived in the Congo had left him doubting his faith.

"You have that same goodness in you," Mason countered with a smile. "But neither of us had the same calling in our heart that Daddy had. He was born to preach the word of God to others. You and I were born to work the orchards."

Jake nodded in agreement.

"Not that I mind helping to spread the Lord's word on mission trips. But it's living the life I have here in Sweet Springs that makes me truly happiest. Speaking of happy," Mason said, "I know I've said this before, but I saw the way you and Addy were interacting that morning I came in when the two of you were having breakfast together. Nothing was different then. She'd still done what she had done, yet you were still able to enjoy her company. The way you used to whenever she'd come back to Sweet Springs to visit Mrs. Tully."

Jake looked away to stare out the window, noting that, like Addy, the deer had fled as well. "I was making the best out of a bad situation."

Mason snorted. "If saying that helps you to sleep at night. But the truth won't just go away by speaking false words."

"What do you want me to say?" Jake asked in frustration.

"I want you to admit, if only to yourself, that your heart wants to forgive Addy, but your stubborn head is determined to hold out."

He couldn't deny his brother's assessment of the situation. His heart had always had a soft spot when it came to Addy. She'd been his boyhood crush, and those feelings had only grown deeper as he'd moved into adulthood, kept alive by the phone calls she made to his momma that he would find his way into being a part of. In the occasional visits she'd made to Sweet Springs over the years, which had been few and far between. Back then, however, he'd been grateful for any time he'd been able to spend with Addy, because being with her, talking to her, always made his heart feel alive. No other woman had ever affected him that way.

Jake looked to his big brother. "Sometimes you know me better than I know myself." That was as close to an admission of truth where his feelings for Addy were concerned as he could muster. It wasn't only his brother he'd never expressed his feelings for Addy to. He'd never let her know where his heart had lain, either, because Addy only thought of him as Mason's little brother, even though only a few years separated them in age. Even as they'd grown older and had developed a true friendship, she'd still referred to him as her good friend and, of course, Mason's younger brother. He'd hoped that with time and patience she would begin to see him as so much more. Had even felt things changing between them. And then Addy had gone and shattered not only his trust with her betrayal…but his heart.

"That's what big brothers are for," Mason told him with an empathetic smile. "Now, how about I go grab us our sandwiches and a few cookies and we can eat while enjoying the view from Finn's window?"

"Would you mind giving me a push outside instead? I'd like to apologize to Addy for making her feel less than welcome when she arrived."

Mason's smile widened into a grin. "I thought you'd never ask." Stepping around Jake, he grabbed onto the chair's rubberized grips and steered it from the room.

Jake ran his apology over in his mind, wishing he were able to walk out to her on his own. The chair and his extended leg definitely slowed them down as his brother maneuvered it into the unfinished hallway and out onto the front porch.

"'Bye!" Finn called out from the edge of the yard where he stood alongside Lila, waving his arm to and fro.

Jake's gaze shifted immediately to the compact pickup truck his sister had recently purchased as it backed down the gravel base that would soon be Mason and Lila's driveway.

Addy returned Finn's wave from where she sat in the passenger side. Then her gaze moved past Lila and Finn to where Jake sat watching her departure from the porch, his unspoken apology sitting heavy on his tongue.

"Jake?" his brother prompted.

"Let them go," he told him with a frown. His apology for Addy was personal, not something he wanted to do in front of a yard full of spectators. So Jake did all he could do at that moment—eyes still locked with Addy's, he offered up a wave of his own as they drove off.

Chapter Eight

Cup of tea in hand, Addy stepped out onto the porch to join Lila, who was enjoying the sun, Peaches curled up on the wicker settee beside her.

"Good morning," Lila greeted cheerily.

"Morning," Addy replied with a yawn.

"Still not sleeping well?"

Addy nodded. When Jake had turned and glanced her way after she'd stopped by the new house with Violet, there had been a flicker of something in his gaze. Regret? Longing? But he'd quickly shuttered his emotions and looked away. It was as if she hadn't even been standing there in the same room. His unspoken rebuff had made her heart ache to the point Addy had needed to leave the situation. Even though she'd felt bad about cutting Violet's visit there so short.

Today, however, Addy had risen from her bed with renewed determination. Jake's momma was right. She had persevered through the toughest of times. She would get through this, too, using that same stubborn determination. She would never give up on her and Jake's friendship. Ever.

"The situation with Jake?" Lila surmised, more a knowing statement than a question.

"Yes," Addy replied. She had prayed more that night than she ever had, except for when Mama Tully had been ill that past summer. It still felt as if she had no right to request anything from the Lord, her not having stepped foot in church since leaving Sweet Springs to go home and live with her momma all those years ago. But the urge to turn to Him in prayer had been strong, and one didn't have to be in the Lord's house to pray. He took all prayers sent Heavenward under consideration. Maybe He would be willing to listen to hers as well. Even if they weren't cast from inside the Lord's House, a place she couldn't imagine entering after so many years.

Addy crossed the porch to where Lila was seated and smiled as she eyed her cat lying there. She smiled again at Lila. "I see that I've been replaced as your bestie."

Lila reached out to stroke the sleeping cat

along her back. "A girl can have two besties, don't you think?"

Addy smiled. "Absolutely. But I thought Mason had already claimed the other spot."

"Hmm…" Lila pretended to contemplate that one. Then she sighed. "I suppose a girl could always have three if she were so blessed."

Her friend *had* been blessed. Although some of those blessings had taken years for Lila to receive.

Lila's gaze dropped to the harvesting basket hooked over Addy's arm. "Are you going to the garden?"

"I am." Their foster mother planted several gardens throughout the year, so there was always a seasonal selection of vegetables to be had. "I asked Mama Tully if I could pick some peas from her fall bounty to add to the pot pie I'm making Jake for lunch today."

Lila's eyes widened in surprise. "Did you just say you were making it for Jake?"

Addy laughed. "I know. That's the last thing you expected to hear from me, but after seeing him at your new house yesterday, my heart tells me there is still a chance at salvaging our friendship."

"He didn't even acknowledge you were there," Lila said with a frown.

"I'm not sure how to explain how I know

there's hope," Addy admitted. "I just know. So I'm going to take Jake the chicken pot pie I had planned to make for him anyway."

"Are you sure about this?" Lila asked worriedly.

"I am," Addy assured her. "I called Jake's momma a few minutes ago to make sure it was all right with her. Like you, she was surprised but happily gave me her blessing to give things with Jake another try."

Lila's worried expression eased into a smile. "Would you like some help picking those peas?"

"I would love that," Addy replied, her mood buoying even more. Her gaze shifted to her beloved cat. "Not sure Peaches is going to appreciate my taking you away from her."

Lila laughed. "Peaches is perfectly content to lie here in the sunshine whether or not I'm sitting here with her." Pushing up from the settee, Lila accompanied Addy off the porch and around the side of the house to the garden.

"This will be just like old times," Addy said, grinning happily as she stepped in among the rows of staked pea plants. When they had fostered there with Mama Tully, they had spent hours helping her plant, care for and then harvest her vegetables. It had been the perfect bonding time. It had also been surprisingly therapeutic. At least for Addy it had.

While she had been helpless to change her own life at that time, she had been able to help watch over and nurture the delicate plants as the seeds sprouted from the rich soil, stretching up toward the sky. Just like Mama Tully had done with her and Lila when they'd come to her as fragile young girls.

"Do you need anything before I head out to the orchard?"

Jake glanced away from the window to see Mason's head poking in around the partially open bedroom door. "As a matter of fact, I do. Would you mind dropping me off at Mama Tully's before heading over to the new house?"

Mason stepped farther into the room. "I'm sorry. I think this door was somehow blocking my hearing. Did you just ask me to—"

"Mason," Jake uttered in frustration. "Can you or can't you?"

"If this involves setting things right with Addy, I'd be more than happy to."

Jake reached for his cell phone, shoving it into the front pocket of his flannel shirt. "I'm not sure if things are going to be set right, but I owe her an apology. I'd like to do so in person."

A wide grin split his brother's face. "Then what are we waiting for?" Grabbing the handles at the back of the wheelchair, he wheeled Jake around and pushed him out of the room.

Mason brought the chair to a stop at the front door and then walked around Jake to open it. As he did, both men gasped in surprise.

"Addy?" Jake managed as his gaze locked with hers through the screen door. Warmth unfurled in his stomach at the sight of her.

She pasted on what looked very much like a nervous smile. "Hello." Then she raised her hand, bringing attention to the deep, foil-covered pie dish she was holding. "I was hoping you might be hungry."

He nodded, still trying to process the fact that Addy was there, standing on his porch. "I never turn down pie. Apple, blackberry, peach—they're all the same to me."

Mason shook his shock off and reached out to open the door. "Sorry," he apologized. "Please, come on in."

"Thank you," she replied, stepping in past Mason to stand next to Jake's chair. Looking down at him, she said, "How about chicken?"

"Chicken?"

She laughed softly. "Pot pie. Fresh out of the oven, using peas from Mama Tully's garden. Lila and I picked them this morning."

Now that she was in the house, he could smell it. Just-baked pie crust. Chicken. Seasonings. Jake's mouth began to water.

"Please tell me Lila made me a pot pie, too," Mason said with a moan.

"Sorry," she told him. "She didn't. But there should be plenty of this one I made to go around."

He nodded and then looked to Jake. "Guess you won't need that ride after all."

"I've caught you at a bad time," Addy said apologetically. She looked down at the dish in her hand. "Why don't I just stick this in the fridge, and you can eat it when you get back?"

"Since I was on my way over to see you, I'd say my plans have just changed."

Her beautiful eyes widened. "You were coming over to see me?"

"I'm going to leave you two to your pot pie and head on over to the house," Mason said, pushing open the screen door. He looked to Jake. "If you need anything, call." Then he smiled. "But I think you're in pretty good hands."

Addy returned his brother's smile.

When Mason eased the front door closed

behind him, Jake looked to Addy. "I was coming over to talk to you about yesterday."

"It was a bit awkward, wasn't it?" she admitted. "If I had known you would be there, I would have declined your sister's invitation. I'm sorry if my being there ruined your outing."

"You had no way of knowing," he replied. "And my being caught off guard was no excuse to be rude. So if anyone is owed an apology, it's you. I should have said hello instead of contemplating how I could manage an escape out the window in this." He motioned to his wheelchair.

She bit back a smile as if unsure whether to be offended or laugh at the direction his thoughts had gone when she'd arrived. "I'm glad you chose to remain and face your enemy."

He frowned. "Addy, you're not my enemy. At least, I don't want you to be."

She made a face that bordered on discomfort. That surprised him. Addy had made it seem like she wanted their friendship to be repaired. Had his behavior the previous day prompted her to have a change of heart?

"Addy?"

"Sorry," she said with a wince, "but the last thing I want to do in the middle of our conversation is walk away, but I really need to set this dish down. It's not long out of the oven, and the heat is starting to seep through the dish towel I have under it."

"Go," he urged, concerned she had burned herself while he'd sat there blathering on.

She didn't need to be told twice. Pot pie in hand, Addy hurried toward the kitchen.

Jake sat waiting, impatience driving him to cast anxious glances in the direction she had gone. Unable to wait any longer, he slid his arm free of its sling and reached for the wheels of his chair.

"What are you doing?" Addy gasped as she came back into view, her gaze fixed on his hands.

"Coming to check on you," he replied.

"I was setting a couple of plates and forks out for us," she told him as she moved to help him get his arm back into his sling. "What were you thinking? You could have caused your injury to worsen instead of heal."

Using his unencumbered arm, he reached for the hand she'd been balancing the pie dish on, turning it over. There was a hint of redness to the pads of her fingers and her palm. The sight of which had Jake frowning. "Does it hurt bad?"

Addy's focus was on their hands. "No," she said more quietly than usual.

"Addy," he pressed.

She lifted her gaze to his. "Only a little. It's more of a light sting as far as pain goes."

Bringing her open hand to his lips, he pressed a gentle kiss to one of the reddened fingertips.

Her breath caught.

He released her hand, smiling up at her.

"Feels better already," she told him, returning his smile. They stood looking into each other's eyes for several long moments before Addy finally looked away. "Let's get you to the kitchen while your lunch is still warm." That said, she moved around to the back of his chair.

"If it hurts to grip the handles, leave me here. We can have a picnic right here."

"Don't be silly," she told him. "My hand is fine." With a nudge, she urged the chair forward.

Minutes later, Jake was settled into his usual chair at the table with Addy seated across from him. But, instead of eating, she was simply pushing the food around on her plate.

"Everything okay?" he asked.

She set her fork down with a sigh. "I hate

to bring up the issues of our past when our time together today has moved in such a positive direction. But I need you to know everything."

He swallowed, the pot pie she'd prepared specially for him catching in his suddenly constricted throat. Jake reached for his glass of sweet tea, wondering what else she might have kept from him. She sounded far too anxious for it to be anything good. He wanted to tell her to leave whatever it was she had to say unspoken so their afternoon wouldn't turn on them the way it had last time.

"I'm all ears," Jake heard himself say, in spite of his reservations, trying to sound unaffected. When she hesitated, he motioned impatiently. "Go ahead. Speak your mind. I'd rather that than have your silence if there's something I need to know."

"*I* need you to know it," she clarified. "Years ago, when Lila showed up unannounced on my family's front doorstep, I knew something was terribly wrong. Her face was tear-streaked and ashen. There were dark circles under her eyes. Apparently, she'd spent several nights in a run-down motel, trying to figure out what to do before coming to me."

Jake hated that Lila had gone through that when she'd had a safe haven right there in

Sweet Springs. But she'd run and placed herself and her unborn child in danger, staying at some seedy motel.

"Lila told me about the baby," Addy went on, "and that she loved Mason too much to ruin his plans to follow in your daddy's footsteps. She couldn't bear the thought of shaming your family, whom she'd come to love so much. I tried to convince her to rethink her decision not to tell Mason about the baby, but she wasn't in a frame of mind to think rationally at that point. She begged me to promise to keep her pregnancy a secret and to never tell Mason, or anyone else, that the baby she was carrying was his."

"You could have refused," he stated simply. "Could have forced Lila to tell us the truth."

"I wanted to," she replied. "But I feared that in her current state of mind Lila could very well have run off again if I didn't give her my word to keep her pregnancy a secret." She paused, tears pooling in her eyes. "I didn't want Lila to end up living life on the streets with her child like Momma had with me for so many years. I didn't want her child to grow up knowing the kind of hunger that would drive a child to beg for scraps of food."

"Addy." He managed to somehow get past the viselike grip her words had on his throat.

He hadn't known what to expect when she'd wanted to open up to him about something, but this made his heart ache for her.

"I didn't want them knowing the ever-present fear that came with living out of a car," she went on, as if she'd held the words in for as long as she could and the emotional dam she'd built up around her was finally giving way. "Or to feel the shame of having to wash up in gas station bathrooms. I knew what it was like to wake from sleep to find some dirty face staring in at me through the car window. And then having to cover my ears to block out the persistent tapping against the glass that separated me from the world outside whenever one of those intrusive strangers sought to coax me to unlock the car door. But I knew better. Momma had told me never to unlock the doors for anyone but her." A lone tear slid down her cheek as those dark memories resurfaced.

Reaching across the table, Jake covered her hand with his in a supportive gesture. "Addy," he said, the huskily spoken word filled with heartfelt empathy.

"Don't," she said firmly, yet she didn't pull away from his gentle touch. "I don't want anyone's pity."

He nodded in understanding, having felt

that way himself, more often than not, after coming home. That's why he hadn't told his family about the true depth of his inner pain. About the tremendous guilt he harbored over the death of his friend. He didn't want their pity. But it was so hard to suppress the emotions hearing about the life she had lived as a child had stirred in him. He hurt for her, for the little girl Addy had been. Felt anger that instead of playing dolls with her friends, she'd been cowering in her car from those who more than likely had wished to cause her harm.

"Where did your momma go that she left you alone in that car to fend for yourself?" Jake asked with a scowl.

"She was never too far away from where our car was parked, but she would be busy, earning money by washing storefront windows, sweeping floors inside those stores, even the sidewalks outside," Addy explained. "When there was no work to be had, Momma would sit on our corner and ask people passing by for their spare change. I would sit there with her in the afternoons, under the shade of the building's overhang. When it got too hot, we would slip inside one of the nearby stores to cool off."

Jake closed his eyes, trying to block out

the image of Addy as a little girl, begging for coins on some street corner. The Good Lord had surely known what He was doing when He'd sent her to live with Mrs. Tully. When Jake opened them, looking to Addy, he noted the faraway look in her pale eyes. He recognized that blank stare. He'd seen it in the mirror many times since coming home. Addy was, no doubt, replaying the painful pieces of her past in her mind. He gave her hand a gentle squeeze, needing her to know he was there for her. Even if only through silent understanding.

Blinking, she looked at him, and her gaze, although misted over, was far more present. "I did what I did," she said, "because I didn't want Finn to grow up like I did."

Amazing how a brief conversation could so completely alter one's way of thinking, bring about such an onslaught of emotions and make one so very grateful for the life God had bestowed upon them. "I'm thankful he didn't have to. Thank you for being there for Lila when she needed you the most."

Surprise lit her face at his response. "I will always be there for her," she replied with a sniffle. "I'm sorry," she muttered as she swiped at the tears sliding down her cheeks with her free hand. "I'm normally not a crier. This is embarrassing."

"You have no reason to be embarrassed. Cry all you want," he told her, his tone gentle and soothing. "I had no idea you'd had to live that way."

"Very few people do," she admitted. "Mama Tully knew when they sent me to her. I opened up to Lila little by little, eventually telling her everything. But it took years for me to share more than just bits and pieces of my past with her. It's not something I care to talk about."

He understood more than she could know. And he wasn't surprised that Addy had taken a while to tell even her best friend about her past. What strength that must have taken for her to speak about that time in her life, to Lila or anyone. How she'd lived in a car, her and her momma scraping by to survive. *A car.* He couldn't even begin to imagine having lived like that, having been raised by two loving parents in a house that offered security and warmth. There had always been food on the table and clean clothes to wear. He'd had siblings to keep the loneliness at bay. And he'd been brought up with a deep-rooted faith that had given him both comfort and direction.

Addy finally pulled her hand away and

lowered her gaze to his plate. "You should eat before your lunch gets cold."

Jake felt her pulling away, locking that raw part of her heart behind that emotional wall that had protected her for so many years. And that was okay. He'd give her the reprieve she needed. When, and if, she was ready to talk more about her past, he would be there to support her.

"Lunch can wait," he told her. "Knowing you're okay is far more important than eating pot pie."

She was more important. Oh, how those words came to Addy like a balm for her aching heart. "Thank you," she said with a soft smile.

"If you ever need to talk, I'm here for you," he said. "I know I haven't been the friend I should have been."

"For good reason," she told him.

"But I was so caught up in my anger toward you, and then after this last devastating mission trip, my guilt, I wasn't emotionally capable of being the man my daddy raised me to be. Addy, I forgive you. I'm sorry it took me so long to do so."

She fought back another surge of tears. Why was it so hard to hold it together when she'd been so strong all her life? As that question came and went, something Jake said took its place. *My guilt.* She looked up at him from across the table. "You were there serving the Lord. You did nothing to deserve that ambush. There's no reason for you to harbor any guilt for what happened."

"Maybe not because of the ambush," he said, sitting back in his chair. "But I feel it deep for being the reason a fellow volunteer I'd befriended died that day."

"Oh, Jake, I'm so sorry," Addy replied. "Lila didn't mention anyone having died."

"My family doesn't know the details of that day," he admitted. "Like you, I decided it was a part of my past better kept locked away."

"Talk to me, Jake," she pleaded. "Opening up to you lifted some of that weight that had been pressing on my heart for so long."

Frowning, he said, "Corey and I were up on a scaffolding working together on one side of the schoolhouse. It was hot, and I was parched. I told him I needed to stop and take a break to grab a bottle of water and asked if he wanted one, too. He did and offered to take over the task I'd been working on while I went to get our drinks. I was only halfway down the ladder when shots rang out." His eyes pinched shut. "He never made it out of the Congo."

"Oh, Jake," she groaned, hurting for him. Her stomach churned as she imagined what that moment had been like for him. The fear and the helplessness he must have felt.

"If I hadn't offered to get us water," Jake said with a slow shake of his head. "If I hadn't switched places with him…"

"Then it would be your family in mourning right now," she said softly. *I would have been mourning your death, too.* Addy could hardly bear the thought of how close she'd come to losing Jake. Losing his friendship was something she could find a way to deal with. But not to death. "I'm so sorry your friend died that day. My heart goes out to the family he left behind. But I'm so grateful you made it home to us."

"Addy, I can't stop thinking about that day. I should have died, not Corey," he said, the words taut with emotion.

"Jake, neither of you should have died that day," she told him. "And while it's been years since I went to church, I know that when it's our time to go be with God, it's our time. The Lord had bigger and better things He needed your friend for."

"I know that," he admitted. "But that doesn't make this any easier to deal with."

"I'm sorry you had to go through something so devastating. Have you thought about talking to someone?"

"I am," he murmured. "I'm talking to you."

"I was referring to a therapist," Addy clarified.

"I don't need professional help," he said with a frown.

"Lila and Mama Tully aren't the only ones who knew about my past before today," she admitted. "I went to see a therapist after I went back to live with Momma again. She and I even went together for a while as we worked toward mending the broken pieces of our relationship. There is no shame in seeking help. Doing so helped me to face a lot of my past. And if not a therapist, then consider talking to Reverend Hutchins."

He was silent for a long moment before finally nodding.

"You will?" she asked, relief washing over her.

"I won't count it out," he told her. "To be honest, opening up to you about what happened has already eased some of that unrelenting pain and guilt I've been feeling."

"I feel the same way," she said with a smile.

"I've missed you."

His admission had both surprise and joy surging through her. "You have?"

He nodded. "More than I wanted to."

Her heart did a hopeful little flip.

"If you have time available while you're still in town," he went on, "and are still willing, I'd like to see about rebuilding our friendship."

"I have the time," she said, sending a silent prayer of thanks Heavenward. "And I'd love to find our way back to where we once were."

He returned her smile. "So would I."

Chapter Nine

"Another delicious lunch," Jake said as Addy rolled him out onto the back porch and down the ramp into the sunshine.

"I'm glad you are enjoying my cooking skills," she replied, and he could hear the smile in her voice.

Jake glanced back over his shoulder at her. "Would you like to take a ride in the Gator?"

She set the brakes and stepped around his chair to face him. "I have a better idea."

"Better than an ATV ride?" he said, pretending to seriously mull the possibilities over.

"Let's just say I think we could have fun doing it," she offered.

"You're taking me skydiving?"

"Not in this lifetime," she said with an adamant shake of her head.

"Because you're afraid of heights?" he asked with a teasing grin.

"That would no doubt come into play," she agreed. "But I think the more obvious obstacle here is the fact that you have a broken leg."

He nodded. "I suppose that could make the landing part a bit rough. I guess that also rules out our going to a trampoline park."

"Jake," she said with a giggle.

He chuckled. "Okay, what's the plan for this afternoon?"

"I thought it might be nice if we went over to the market and gave your momma a hand with things over there."

His boyish grin sagged. "Addy, I'm stuck in this wheelchair and have one arm in a sling. How much help can I be?"

"There are a lot of things you can do to help her out," she told him. "Like printing labels and seeing to some of the market's accounting paperwork. You could even offer to have your momma place the heavier boxes on your lap and then push you to wherever she needs to restock in the store, instead of her having to carry them herself. Some of them can be pretty heavy."

His frustration eased at her words. "I could do that," he decided with a nod.

"You can do anything you set your mind to, Jake Landers," she told him.

"You make me feel that way," he said as they started across the yard.

Addy smiled, her heart soaking up his words.

"I've been so caught up in what I can't do since coming home," Jake said, "that I never stopped to consider what I could do. Like helping out Momma." He sighed. "I should have thought of this myself."

"You needed rest to help you regain your strength after you came home," she reminded him. "But you're growing stronger every day."

"It does feel like I've turned a corner."

Thank the Lord for that.

Addy pushed the chair up onto the market's porch, using the handicap access ramp, excited to be getting Jake to be more involved in the family business. She knew how much he'd missed contributing to it during his recovery. Stopping just outside the door, she stepped around the chair and knelt before him. "You are here to help now," she said softly. "And your momma is going to be so excited to have you working with her. So stop wasting your energy on woulda, coulda, shouldas. Lord knows we both have done far too much of that, because wishing it so isn't going to change the past."

Jake's mouth curled up into a smile. "Has anyone ever told you how pretty you are when you're determined to get a point across?"

Pretty? Jake thinks I'm pretty? Shaking her head, Addy said with an embarrassed smile, "No."

"Well, now you have."

Addy fought to control her reaction to his unexpected compliment, seeing as how she suddenly felt as giddy as a schoolgirl inside. Maybe Lila was right in her assessment of Addy's heart. She took in the man seated in the wheelchair before her. Although temporarily laid low by his injuries, Jake Landers was still a man of strength, tall like his brother and broad-shouldered. And quite handsome.

"Uh, do I have something on my face?" Jake asked with a grin as he took a swipe over his mouth with his free hand. "Mayonnaise from my sandwich, maybe? I did have a little trouble using the squirt bottle with my less dominant hand."

Addy pulled her gaze away from his face, feeling her cheeks warm as she straightened. "Your face is just fine," she answered as she turned to open the door.

"I thought you'd never notice," he muttered behind her.

Addy didn't have to see his face to know that Jake was grinning from ear to ear. She felt a tug at her own mouth as she reached out to open the market's front entry door.

It opened on its own, startling Addy.

"Well, hello, you two," Mrs. Landers greeted them with a delighted grin. "I didn't expect to see you here today."

"Addy suggested we come over and lend a hand for a bit this afternoon," Jake told her.

She looked to Addy. "That was sweet of you." Her gaze swung back to Jake. "But are you sure you're up for it? You're welcome to just visit if you like. We're slow today, so I'm working on restocking some of our fall products."

"I'm not here to visit," Jake told her, exchanging a glance with Addy. "I'm here to help with whatever I can."

Addy smiled, hearing the newfound confidence in his tone. She had helped to give him that and it made her feel so good inside. Not to mention how proud she was of Jake for pushing past the darkness that had been swallowing him up and taking this step toward getting his life back.

"Well, come on in," his momma said, stepping aside so that Addy could push Jake's chair into the building. "I was just running over to the house to box up those pies I made last night. The ones Mason carried over for me this morning are nearly gone."

"I'd be happy to go get them for you," Addy offered.

"You two just got here," Mrs. Landers said. "I'll run over. I want to grab my sweater anyway. It gets a bit chilly in the market with the air on. I forgot to bring it over with me this morning. Be right back."

Addy then turned to close the door behind his momma. When she swung back around to face Jake, she found him staring off into the market as if he'd never seen it before.

"You okay?" she asked.

"I've always taken this place for granted, because it's been in the family for as long as I can remember. To think it took nearly dying to realize how much the orchard and this market really mean to me." He shook his head and added with a bit more of a pull to his voice, "I came so close to never being here again."

"Thank the Lord you are," Addy said, his reminder of how close she came, they all came, to losing him, bringing a sting of tears to her eyes. To think that he might have died without knowing just how very much he meant to her.

When he fell silent, Addy glanced Jake's way. "Speaking of God, your momma told me you haven't been going to church with them. Is it because of Corey?"

He frowned. "It was a senseless death. Corey was there to serve God. So, yes, I've not been in a good place since coming home when it comes to my relationship with God."

Just like her own momma. Yet not. Jake had been raised with a strong Christian family and beliefs. Her momma hadn't been. For Addy, not going to church was something she'd accepted for her momma's sake. But for him to turn away from the Lord filled Addy with so much sadness for him.

"Jake," she said gently, her voice filled with compassion. "God isn't to blame for the evil that happens in the world." It was the same thing she'd said to her momma after they'd been reunited, but words couldn't change her momma's way of thinking. But Jake, coming from the family he did, had to know it for the truth it was. "That's something I learned attending your daddy's Sunday services when I lived here. Church is a place to find healing. To find comfort. To find hope."

He looked up at her, one lone brow lifting. "If you feel that way in your heart, why haven't you been attending services with Mama Tully during your visit here?"

The question took her aback, even though she'd just pressed him about the very same thing. Lila had been trying to convince Addy to get back to church ever since she'd reconciled with Mason and renewed her own faith that past summer. "Did your momma say something about my not going?" Worry filled her. Had she disappointed Mrs. Landers yet again by not attending Sunday services?

"Not Momma. Finn," he answered before she could finish her question. "He was talking about the windows at the front of the church because they were all different colors, but that his aunt Addy doesn't visit the Lord's house. She prays at home instead."

"I rarely even do that," she admitted with a sigh. "Truth is, I haven't been to church since leaving Sweet Springs because Momma blamed God for all our struggles. I tried to explain to her that God hadn't made the bad things happen to us. That through those times He'd watched over us. Without Him, we might not have even had a car to shelter in or food when true hunger set in."

Jake hung his head, giving it a shake, and then lifted his gaze to her. "Your inner strength amazes me. All you went through and you still opened your heart to the Lord, even coming to His defense at the risk of going against your momma's family's beliefs."

"I didn't cling to my faith the way I should have," she confessed. "I decided it was better not to bring religion into my relationship with Momma. It would only cause strife when all I wanted was to fit into our new life together. When I finally moved out into my own place, bringing Lila and Finn with me, I felt like I was too far removed from the faith I'd found here in Sweet Springs to attempt to reconcile with the Lord."

"It's never too late to find your way back to God," Jake told her.

"I'm working on it," she told him. It hadn't been something she'd given much thought to in Atlanta. Not after so many years away from the faith she'd known only briefly. But after Mama Tully had gotten sick that past summer, she'd found herself asking God to heal her foster mother. And then she'd come back to Sweet Springs to find Jake injured, and her prayers had turned to asking for his recovery as well. "The Good Lord has probably been working overtime, given the amount of prayers I've sent up in the past few months."

"You put me to shame," he said. "What happened during my mission trip was life-changing and, beyond a doubt, faith-testing. I'm man enough to admit that I haven't handled things the way a man of faith should have. That's something I need to set to rights." He looked up, meeting her gaze. "Would you consider going to church with me this coming Sunday?"

"Yes," she said, emotion clogging her throat. This wouldn't be easy for either of them, but it would be so much better stepping into that church together, supporting one another. "It's long past time for me to take back what I gave up for Momma's sake."

The market door opened, and Addy glanced past Jake to offer a welcoming smile.

Jake glanced back over his shoulder, immediately offering a friendly grin of his own. "Reverend."

If this wasn't a sign from Heaven, Addy didn't know what was. She'd met the reverend a time or two during her visits to Sweet Springs to see Mama Tully. "Hello, Reverend Hutchins. Are you looking for anything special? Jake's momma ran over to the house, but we would be more than happy to help you find whatever it is you were looking for."

His gaze drifted to one of the room's side

windows, the one facing Jake's house. "I, uh, think I'll just look around for a bit, if that's all right."

"Just holler if you need anything," Addy told him.

"I will," he replied. "Thank you."

"He's going to buy a pie," Jake whispered after the reverend had walked away.

Addy leaned in, asking softly, "How do you know that?"

"Because he comes in at least once a week, every week, to buy one of Momma's pies."

"He does?" Addy said, her focus shifting back to the reverend.

The door swung open, and Mrs. Landers hurried into the market as if swept in by a strong gust of wind. "I'm back."

As if sent over by that same burst of wind, Reverend Hutchins was there reaching for the stack of pie boxes. "Here, let me get those for you."

A bright smile moved across her face. "Thank you," she said, handing them over. "Would you mind carrying them back to the bakery?"

"Not at all. I was just perusing your assortment of jellies."

Addy stood watching the interaction, wondering if the reverend came by each week for reasons other than purchasing a peach pie. After all, he was unmarried and had offered emotional support to Mrs. Landers after Jake's daddy had passed away, and he'd been a part of their lives for years. Whatever the reverend's reason for being there, it had effectively put a spring back in Mrs. Landers's step. That did Addy's heart good. She'd been worried about Jake's momma, seeing her try and take care of everyone but herself. But then Addy wasn't much different. She'd always tried to do for others rather than focusing on her own needs. This trip home had her realizing how important it was to find things that brought her joy as well. Like spending time with Jake.

"Penny for your thoughts," Jake said as he watched Addy watching his momma with a soft smile.

She looked his way, her smile widening. "I'm not sure you want to know what I was thinking about just now."

"Try me."

"I think the reverend is sweet on your momma," she said, so quietly he almost missed what she'd said.

"What?" he said with a muffled snort.

"Jake," she warned in a hush.

Laughter erupted at the back of the store. His momma's and the reverend's joyous laughter. Head snapping around, Jake zeroed in on the two now gathered around the handcrafted fork chimes that hung suspended from a wire tree.

"I think she might return the sentiment."

At that, Jake turned back to Addy. "Momma is friendly with everyone. Besides, Reverend Hutchins is a preacher."

"Who's also a man," she said as if he needed reminding of that fact at this moment. Not when he was looking at his momma, who seemed to be oblivious to anyone or anything else but the happy conversation she was caught up in with Reverend Hutchins.

"She's older than him," he said, figuring that was a good point to make. But the moment the words were out of his mouth, Jake wanted to pull them back.

"And that makes him off-limits?"

He looked up into her questioning eyes, thinking about their own age difference. Not that a few years made much difference now that they were adults. Not as much as it had when they were teenagers. And it certainly hadn't kept him from falling in love with her.

Love?

If he hadn't been seated in a wheelchair,

Jake would have taken a step back. There was so much going on in his head right then. An unexpected upheaval of his emotions. First, realizing that his momma's heart could actually be needing something more. Something he felt at peace with if that really were the case. And second, realizing that his own heart needed something more—*Addy*.

"I could be wrong," Addy said.

"You might not be," he told her as his momma and Reverend Hutchins made their way to the front of the store.

"I'll walk you out," his momma offered.

"I need to pay for my pie first," the reverend reminded her.

She smiled. "This one's on the house."

"You worked hard to make this delicious pie," he replied. "I insist on paying you for it."

"All right," his momma relented and led him over to the cash register.

Jake looked to Addy, who was giving him one of those I-told-you-so kind of looks he usually received from one of his siblings.

With a ding of the cash register drawer closing, his momma stepped back around the counter to accompany Reverend Hutchins outside.

"Good seeing you both," he said with a

departing wave to Addy and Jake as they passed by.

"You'll be seeing us both again in church this Sunday," Addy called out after him.

Mrs. Landers stopped in the doorway with a soft gasp. "He will?" she said, her eyes alight with joy.

Jake grinned. "He will." It was time he leaned on the faith he'd grown up with and stopped blaming God for the bad that had happened that day in the Republic of Congo. Maybe in doing so he could finally start to heal emotionally.

"Thanks for riding into town with me," Addy said as she pulled into an empty parking space in front of The Flower Shack. She had begun to look forward to their outings with eager anticipation, instead of the dread she'd felt in the beginning whenever she was around Jake.

"It's not like I had other plans," Jake reminded her.

She offered up a sympathetic smile. "You are going to be back to your usual antics before you know it. For now, you need to accept that your body is still healing and be patient with it."

"Easier said than done," he grumbled.

"Has anyone ever told you how adorable you are when you're pouting?" And when he was smiling. And when he was lost in thought.

Jake straightened in the seat as if being adorable took away from his manliness. "I'm not pouting."

Reaching down, Addy released her seat belt and then reached for the door handle. "Whatever you say."

"So you think I'm adorable?" he called after her as she stepped from the car.

With a shake of her head, Addy closed the door and walked around to help Jake into his wheelchair.

"I seem to have missed your reply," he teased as he settled himself into the chair.

"That's because I didn't answer you," she told him as she stepped around to push him into the flower shop. She knew if she did she might say more than he was prepared to hear. That she adored everything about him. That he made her want to feel instead of keeping her emotions guarded.

"So it's a yes," he persisted.

Addy burst into laughter. "Talk about needy."

The shop door swung open just then, and Braden stepped outside. "Saw you pull up from the window," he said as he strode in their direction. "Here, let me get that," he offered.

Addy let go of the chair's grips. "Violet didn't tell me you were working today."

"I'm not," Braden replied. "I just stopped by to see how things were going."

"Perfectly, I'm sure," Jake said as his best friend pushed him inside. "Violet doesn't do anything halfway."

"She's pretty independent," Braden said.

"That's Braden's nice way of saying my sister is too stubborn for her own good," Jake clarified.

"Must run in the family," Addy replied with a grin, making Braden chuckle.

"She's got you pegged," he told Jake.

Jake glanced her way. "I'd say she knows me better than most."

Addy smiled. The same went for Jake. He knew more about her than even her therapist had. At least when it came to the silly little things that made up who she was. Like how she preferred crunchy peanut butter to regular. Or how she tended to hum while baking in the kitchen. And she hadn't forgotten how much he enjoyed identifying the different species of birds and listening to them sing. Or how much he loved entertaining children with really bad magic tricks during the town's various festivities, which Jake would always tell her all about during their phone conversations. Funny how she'd never really given any thought to just how much they really knew about each other.

"Was there anything in particular you were looking for?" Braden asked them.

"I'm picking up a half dozen dahlias to use in the photos of the recipe I'm making this evening for the cookbook." She glanced around. "Violet set them aside for me."

"She's out back overseeing the unloading of a fresh flower delivery," Braden explained before going to get her.

Moments later, Violet hurried into the room. "Sorry to keep you waiting."

"We didn't mind," Addy assured her.

Violet looked to her brother and smiled. "It's good to see you getting out."

"Addy gets all the credit for that," he admitted. "I had planned to hang around the house and work on crossword puzzles all day."

His sister laughed. "You did not. I've never seen you do a crossword puzzle in your life."

"He was actually working on a new design for the orchard's watering system," Addy said.

"Tinkering was all," he countered.

"Still, it's good to know that you're getting back to some of the things you love to do," Violet said as she walked over to pull a wrapped bundle from the oversize floral cooler. "Always building something or looking for ways to improve something that already exists." She handed the flowers Addy had ordered over to her. "I tried to pick out the most perfect ones, since I know you wanted to use them in your pictures."

Addy looked them over. "These are beautiful. And the colors will really pop alongside the butter pecan pound cake I'm making." She reached into her cross-body bag and pulled out her wallet. "I might need a few more for my last recipe, but I'm not sure how I want to present it yet."

"I'm sure you'll figure it out," Violet replied. "But if you need any help, just give me a call."

The door to the back opened and Braden stepped back into the main shop. "Delivery is all taken care of."

Violet smiled up at him. "Thank you."

"Anytime," he offered with a grin.

Addy smiled. "I guess your brother and I had better get going and let you get back to work. Thanks again for picking these out special for my cookbook."

Jake's sister smiled. "Anytime."

"Let me help you out," Braden offered.

"I've got him," Addy said, stepping around behind Jake's chair.

"Okay," he said. "Let me at least get the door for you." He hurried across the room to open it for them.

"I can't wait until I'm not depending on everyone to do even the simplest of things for me," Jake muttered with a frown. "Opening doors, driving, you name it."

"Don't worry, Jake," Addy told him as she pushed him from the store. "When I come home in the spring for the wedding, you can do all those things for me."

Braden and Violet's infectious laughter followed them to the car.

Addy couldn't help but smile. It felt wonderful to be back around so many people she cared about. Around the laughter and the love.

"They might be laughing," Jake said as he settled into the car, "but I intend to do just that and more."

As she stood looking down at his handsome face, seeing the sweet determination in his eyes, the image of a perfect little rustic country house complete with a white picket fence drifted into her mind. Addy took a step back, her heart pounding. Standing on the porch had been none other than Jake Landers.

Knocked a bit off-kilter by that all too vivid image, Addy managed a nervous smile. "You don't owe me anything for helping you. I'm doing it because I want to." Closing the door, she rounded the car. She did so because she cared about him. More than that. She loved him. Not as Mason's little brother, as she'd long tried to make herself believe. She loved him as the man he'd grown into. Not that she was prepared to express those feelings to Jake or anyone else. The realization was all too new And their lives were rooted in two different places. Hers in Atlanta, hopefully working for another highly rated hotel. She was still waiting to hear back on several job applications she'd submitted since coming to Sweet Springs.

Jake's life was here in this wonderful little town where everyone knew everyone. Where he could do all those things he loved. Like work the family orchards, take rides through the woods and over the countryside on his ATV, fish in the pond at the back side of their property and work side by side with his brother to keep the orchard producing and the market updated. Even if her career didn't hold her to a more populated area, there were so many other reasons a relationship wasn't in the future for them. Her part in keeping Finn from his family. And despite his recent step back from his deeply ingrained beliefs, one he was setting right, his life was faith-based, where hers had nothing more than an occasional prayer cast Heavenward. He deserved so much more than she was able to offer him.

"Addy, I'll be doing it because I want to do it, too." *Because I'm pretty sure I'm in love with you.* The declaration remained unspoken. The truth of it too newly realized. Too complicated.

She flashed him a smile before turning her focus to the road as they pulled out onto the main street of town. "I'm going to miss this place when I go back to Atlanta. When I've come home before, I've only stayed for two or three nights. Being here for weeks has made it feel more like it did when I used to live here. So comfortable. So…"

She paused, and Jake found himself waiting eagerly for her next words.

"Right," Addy said.

One word. But it was the best word she could have spoken when describing how being back in Sweet Springs felt to her. It almost gave him hope that maybe someday she might consider moving back. Almost. Sweet Springs didn't offer her much in the way of her career. The town was too small. Her opportunities too limited. He nodded. "I know what you mean. I've traveled a good bit, mostly on mission trips to other countries, but there's no place that's ever made me want to put down roots like this quiet little town I grew up in."

"I only spent a few years here as a teen, but I know what you mean. I do love this wonderfully warm little town." Addy's cell rang, cutting into their conversation. She glanced in Jake's direction. "Would you mind if I take this? I don't recognize the number, so it might be in response to one of the job applications I submitted."

"Not in the least," he assured her. "I'll just enjoy the passing scenery outside." He looked away, trying to give her at least the feel of privacy when sitting side by side in a car was anything but.

"Addy Mitchell," she answered as the call switched over to her car audio system.

"Ms. Mitchell," a male voice on the other end replied, "this is Ed Johnson with Malamar Properties."

"Yes, hello."

"I'm calling in response to your job application, which I must say was quite impressive."

"Thank you."

Jake felt his heart sink. He knew what this call might mean for her, but for him it could be the end of the future he'd begun to see for them. But the man was right. Addy was the best of the best when it came to creating recipes and baking. Throw in her skill for managing people and she was a shoo-in for any pastry chef management position.

"Unfortunately, we've chosen a different applicant to fill the position," he said in a businesslike manner. "We do, however, appreciate your taking the time to consider our hotel in your job search."

"I see," she said, and it took everything in Jake not to glance her way. He'd let her finish her call first. "Thank you for calling to let me know."

"You're welcome," he replied. "Have a good rest of your afternoon."

Addy disconnected the call. "Well, one down. Four more to go."

Jake looked her way. A moment ago, he might have wanted to celebrate this outcome. But instead he felt disappointment for her. Her happiness meant everything to him. Even if it didn't align with his own dreams. "I'm sorry," he began and only then realized she was smiling. "Addy?"

She looked his way as if that call had never happened. "Yes."

Was she hiding her emotions because he was in the car? Addy had always guarded her emotions well. "Are you okay?"

"I am, actually," she said, as if surprised by the fact.

"I take it that wasn't one of your top choices?"

They turned, heading out of town. "I thought it was," she admitted. "But when he told me I didn't get the job, I was surprisingly relieved. I know it doesn't make a lick of sense, especially when I submitted my résumé to them with the hopes of being hired on."

"Maybe it's not what you want to be doing," he surmised. "Or where you want to be." He wished that last part hadn't sounded so hopeful. But maybe it was possible that she'd be happier staying in Sweet Springs and finding work in the area.

"I can't imagine doing anything else," she told him. "I love being a pastry chef. Love creating new recipes. Especially those revolving around dessert."

"Have you ever considered going out on your own? Maybe opening a bake shop?"

Addy laughed. "Have I ever? Only a zillion times. But to start up something like that in Atlanta would require a lot of money. While I have a good bit saved and have the cash from my severance package I could use, it's just not an option. I would never risk running my savings down."

He nodded in understanding. Knowing what he did now about Addy's life growing up, he could imagine how important it was for her to have that financial security. He admired her for wanting more than she'd had growing up, for working so hard to make that happen.

"Maybe your cookbook will really take off and give you more financial freedom to realize your dreams."

"Wouldn't that be nice?" she said with a smile.

"Maybe we'll order some to sell in The Perfect Peach."

Her face lit up. "That's so sweet," she said, deeply touched that he'd followed through.

"Absolutely," he replied with a grin. "I mean, I was a big contributor to this cookbook, being your recipe taster and all."

"True. Hmm…"

"Hmm…what?"

"I'm just thinking I need to add an acknowledgment page to let the world know how much I appreciate your putting your stomach on the line to sample my new recipes. Oh, and I'll have to acknowledge Finn, too," she added.

"Without a doubt," Jake agreed with a chuckle. It felt so good to be able to laugh again. To set some of his emotional pain aside. Addy had been a big part of that, truly leading by example, and he was so grateful she'd determinedly forced her way back into his life after he'd shut her out.

They turned onto the road leading to the orchard. "Do you need a ride to therapy tomorrow?"

Jake shook his head. "No, but thanks for the offer. Braden's taking me to my session, and then we're going to grab some lunch and catch up."

"Then I guess I'll see you at church on Sunday," she said as she pulled up to the house.

"See me?"

Her head snapped around, worry creasing her brow. "You're not going?"

"Oh, I plan on it, but I thought we were going to do this together. That is, if you don't mind picking me up."

She placed the car in Park and then turned to face him. "I don't mind. In fact, having you there with me when I walk through those open church doors will help give me the courage I know I'm going to need."

Jake smiled. "Addy, keep in mind that those doors are open in welcome. God's house is for everyone who chooses to enter it."

"Thank you for saying that," she told him.

"They're not just words," he told her. "The Lord does forgive. I believe that in my heart."

The front door opened, and Mason stepped out onto the porch with a wave.

Jake groaned. "I told him I would call when I was ready for him to take me up to the house." He wasn't even close to ready. He would sit there until night fell talking to Addy if he could. But she had a recipe to work on, and he'd promised Mason he would help with plans for building a fort for Finn in the new backyard, complete with a rope ladder and a kid-size rock wall.

Reaching down, Addy popped the trunk so Mason could grab Jake's wheelchair. "I'm sure your brother's anxious to get to work on those plans. You're so good at envisioning things that don't exist and making them a reality. I can't wait to see what you two come up with when I come back for the wedding."

He didn't want to think about her leaving, but that's all he seemed to think about lately. How each day was one day closer to not having her right next door. How seeing her smile over a video chat could never compare with the warmth it exuded in person. "I look forward to showing it to you when you come home." Reaching down, he opened the door.

"I'll see you Sunday morning," Addy said as he worked his way out of the car and into the waiting wheelchair.

"I look forward to it," he replied.

"And Jake…" she called out.

He dipped his head to look inside, meeting her gaze.

"There's nobody I'd rather have by my side when I reclaim my faith than you."

"Same," he said with a tender smile before closing the door.

Mason backed the chair away from the car as Addy pulled away. "Are you ready for me to push you inside? Or would you prefer to sit here watching Addy's car go until it disappears from sight?" his brother asked, his tone teasing. "Because that's the kind of thing we men do when we're mooning over a girl."

"I suppose this broken leg is my saving grace," Jake admitted. "Or else I might have gone so far as to run after her down the road, professing my undying love."

Mason threw his head back with a chuckle. "Now that I would have loved to see."

"Come on," Jake said, inclining his head in the direction of the house. "Let's go get that big-boy adventure play set drawn up." As they turned to start for the house, he found himself sneaking just one more glance of Addy's car as it disappeared from sight.

Chapter Ten

Addy reached down, fruitlessly trying to brush the dirt from the front of her cotton skirt, as she stood outside her car. Then she straightened, her gaze straying across the church parking lot to the building where she had long ago learned to worship. Where had the week gone, that it was Sunday already? Her stomach felt twisted up in knots. Maybe if they weren't running late, she'd have less anxiety. But this was a big day for both her and Jake. One that hadn't started off so well. She prayed it wasn't a sign from the Lord, telling her that the welcome mat to His house, the church she was eyeing apprehensively from the parking lot, was not meant for her.

Taking a deep breath, she rounded the car to get Jake's wheelchair out of the trunk.

The passenger door opened, and Jake unfolded his six-foot frame until he was standing there, balancing on one leg.

"Jake," she gasped as she hurried over to him, "what are you doing?"

"Saving time," he replied with his usual disarming smile. "I promise I didn't put any weight on my bad leg."

"You better not have," she muttered as he lowered himself into the chair. "Your momma would have my hide if you undid all the healing that's been done."

"You okay, Addy?" he said, growing serious. "I mean, I know this morning hasn't gone as smoothly as we'd like, but we're here now."

She looked toward the church again. "We're here now," she repeated and then looked down at Jake. "Is it bad that I'm wishing I hadn't changed that tire as quickly as I did? I'm not sure if I'm ready for this."

"We've got this," he told her, reaching out with his unbound arm to take her hand in his, giving it a supportive squeeze.

She glanced down at their joined hands and then back up into Jake's clean-shaven and undeniably handsome face. "Yes, we do." When she was with Jake, she felt like she could face anything, do anything.

Releasing her hand, he settled back against

his wheelchair. "You do realize that Momma is probably sitting in church right now, convinced we changed our minds about coming this morning."

Addy nodded in agreement and moved behind him to push the chair up the ramp. "I think you're right. Your momma didn't sound the least bit convinced when she called to see where we were and you told her a flat tire had us running late for Sunday service." Jake's phone had been on speaker when he called to let his momma know what was going on. There had been no missing the hint of disappointment in his momma's voice when she'd said she hoped they make it for at least part of that morning's service. Looking down at her outfit, she said with a laugh, "Luckily, we have proof of our misadventure this morning."

"I'm not sure ruining your nice skirt because you had to change a tire would be considered lucky by most people," Jake pointed out with a shake of his head. "But I will say that I was very impressed with your ability to change a tire faster than a professional racing pit crew while in not only a skirt but heels as well."

She laughed at his exaggeratory compliment, but it tickled her that her actions had impressed him. That he appreciated her ability to handle certain situations that arose, because she had worked so hard to never again be that helpless little girl. "I didn't mind doing it. I've been seeing to my own tire changes since buying my first car. I can even change my own oil but prefer to go somewhere to have it done for me."

Jake glanced back at her over his shoulder. "I'm just sorry I wasn't able to take care of that flat tire for you. I'll buy you a new skirt."

"I'm not worried about my skirt," she told him. "And I don't think the Lord is going to mind a few smudges of dirt on my Sunday best. It's proof that God is good, giving us a safe place to pull over and change our tire. And it's not raining, despite the morning news having called for a shower or two."

He glanced back at her again. "You, Adeline Mitchell, are a truly amazing woman."

"Must be why we get along so well," she told him with a warm smile. "You're pretty amazing yourself."

They entered the sanctuary just as the congregation stood to sing one of that morning's scheduled hymns and the organ played. Addy had always loved listening to the instrument. It was so powerful, sparking life into every single note lifting Heavenward through those pipes. The sound was undeniably moving to one's soul.

Addy eased the chair to a stop, her gaze searching the church. As if sensing their arrival, Mama Tully cast a glance back, catching sight of Addy and Jake at the rear of the church. She nodded with a smile as she continued singing. She was seated with Lila, Finn and the rest of the Landers family a few rows back from where Reverend Hutchins stood at the pulpit, his face animated with joy as he joined in the heartfelt singing.

Fearing that Jake might be uncomfortable trying to get himself out of the wheelchair, Addy bent down to whisper, "Would you mind very much if we take these empty seats right here at the back of the church? I'd feel better easing into things this morning."

He nodded his reply. Moments later Addy was seated next to Jake in the last pew, his wheelchair folded up and tucked securely away.

When the music ended, Reverend Hutchins welcomed everyone to that morning's service and announced that the day's sermon was going to be about courage.

Such a fitting topic to begin their return to the Lord with, Addy thought. It had taken courage to go through the things they had and not break completely. It took courage for Jake to forgive her and for Addy to forgive herself. It took courage to step into God's house after having forsaken Him.

Addy glanced over to see Jake with his eyes closed. This time it was her hand moving to cover his. It took courage to love as well.

"Glad you made it to church this morning," Mason told Jake, reaching for the basket of biscuits on the table in front of him. Then he looked to Addy. "Thank you."

"For what?" she replied in confusion.

"For getting my brother to rejoin the world around him," Violet said as she stabbed at a chunk of pot roast, placing it onto her plate.

"And to come back to his roots and attend church again," his momma chimed in with a happy smile as she passed a dish of southern-style green beans to Mrs. Tully, who was seated next to her at the table. "To be honest, until I stepped outside to call you, I worried you might have changed your mind about attending this morning's services."

"We figured you might have thought that," Jake said, exchanging a glance with Addy. "We would have called or texted but knew that everyone would have their phones off."

"Daddy didn't," Finn piped up before stuffing a forkful of fried potatoes into his mouth. "He was sending hearts to Momma on his phone."

Jake nearly choked on the drink of lemonade he'd just taken. He looked to Mason, whose face had taken on a bit more color than normal.

Lila giggled. "Which I didn't see until after church when *I* turned my phone back on."

"In my own defense," Mason said, "I shut my phone off as soon as the music began."

"Hearts," Jake said with a grin as he returned to eating.

"I think it's sweet," Addy said in Mason's defense. Oh, how she'd missed this. She hadn't joined in one of their family after–Sunday service meals since she'd fostered there. "It's those little things a man does that lets a woman know she's never far from your thoughts."

Mason's brows lifted, a smug smile spreading across his face. "Take note, little brother. I have what is known as swag."

Jake rolled his eyes. He was not the heart-and-flower-texting kind of guy. But maybe he should be. He glanced toward Addy, wondering if she would appreciate those little love-sick emoticons, too? Because if it would put a smile on her face, maybe even make her day, he would definitely reconsider his stance on the silliness of it.

"Jake," Lila said, drawing his attention her way, "you might also make note of the importance of proofreading any texts you might send to that special someone." She looked to Mason. "While heart emojis are quite romantic, having them followed by the words I lobe you makes it all just a little bit less special."

"Love," Mason blurted out. "I love you."

Lila reached up to pinch Mason's cheek playfully. "And I love you, too."

"Oh, how I've missed this," Addy announced as she looked around the table. "Dinner with Momma and my stepdaddy have never been like yours. The desserts definitely couldn't compare with the ones you serve."

"Speaking of desserts," Jake's momma said to Addy, "how is that cookbook of yours coming along?"

"Faster than expected," she replied, her posture perking up at the mention of her beloved project. "I just have one more recipe I want to add to it, but it's not quite right. I'm going to work on it again tomorrow. Hopefully, I can get it figured out." Her smile widened. "It's hard to believe it's finally going to happen. In two weeks or so, my very own cookbook will be available for people to buy."

"You should be very proud of yourself," Jake's momma said.

"I know we are," Mrs. Tully chimed in, her statement followed by the bobbing of heads all around the dining room table.

"If you need any help with that last recipe, I'm available," Jake told her, looking for any excuse to spend more time with Addy. He also wanted to be a part of her realizing this dream. To see the pride and joy on her face when that last recipe was perfected.

"Thanks, Jake," Addy replied with a smile. "You've been so much help already."

Mason grinned. "It's not like it's been a real hardship for my brother, getting to taste all those sweet confections you come up with."

"Not in the least," Jake agreed, his focus fixed on Addy. "Look, I know it's not your day to come over tomorrow, but we've got a big kitchen here. I'm sure Momma wouldn't mind us doing a little cooking in here."

"Not in the least," his momma agreed. "Violet and I are going to be busy at the market all day putting up holiday decor."

The Perfect Peach's most popular piece of decor was the life-size animated snowman, or as it was, the peachman, which he and Mason had painted in varying shades of red and peach at their momma's request. Christmas had always been her favorite holiday. His too, because of all it represented. More now than ever before, having gone through what he had. He only wished Addy's stay could be through the year's end so they could share in the joy together.

"I appreciate the offer," Addy said to both Jake and his momma. "But I'd hate to make a mess of your kitchen."

"That's what kitchens are for," his momma replied. "To create messes in. To bake to your heart's content in. And to gather with those you love in."

Addy's gaze flicked to him and then back to his momma, sending a surge of warmth to Jake's heart. Was it possible Addy felt the same special pull between them? He found himself praying more and more for the same kind of happiness his brother had found with Lila. After years of being content to be a bachelor, his focus on the orchard, Jake felt his heart suddenly yearning for more. For Addy, who was like living sunshine, lighting up his days. Always making him smile. She had helped to bring him back from a very dark place, had made him truly appreciate not only the second chance at life God had given him but his life in general. She was a true blessing in his life. His heart's true love.

"If you're sure," she told his momma and then looked to Jake, "and if you don't have other plans, then I'd love to have your help with this last recipe."

He smiled. "I'm more than sure. Besides, I've tasted your culinary creations. There's no way I'd ever turn down the opportunity to serve as taste tester for one of your recipes." Especially knowing that she intended to donate some of her earnings to a charity. He loved that about her, her giving, caring side. They both devoted time to helping others in need, making him feel even more connected to her.

"And if this cookbook does well…" Lila prompted, glancing in Addy's direction.

"If it does well?" Mrs. Landers pressed.

"I was thinking about putting a second cookbook together and donating a portion of those sales to your church's future mission trips."

"Addy," Jake's momma said, pressing a hand to her heart, "that's so generous of you."

Heads bobbed in agreement around the table.

"It really is," Jake said, feeling a small surge of anxiety. He'd always looked forward to mission trips, for the chance to serve the Lord. And then the Congo had happened.

Forcing his rising fear from his thoughts, he called on his faith to give him strength. Because he refused to let the darkness that had happened that day keep him from sharing the light of God's love.

"Coming home," she went on, "being surrounded by all of you, with your deep faith and generosity to others, has made me realize how much I've missed being a part of that."

She could be, Jake thought to himself. He wanted nothing more than for Addy to move back to Sweet Springs permanently. To sit beside him in church. To share laughter with him. To watch old Westerns with him. To love him.

"You're generous, sweetie," Mama Tully said.

"But not when it comes to God," Addy admitted with a frown. "I should be doing my part in helping to spread His word to others. If not through mission trips, then through my gift of cooking, raising additional funds through a cookbook I put together."

The mission program through his family's church had been a part of their lives for as long as Jake could remember. It had begun with their daddy, who had taken part in several shorter mission trips when he and his siblings were younger. After he'd taken over as the church's head pastor, Mason and Jake had volunteered for their first mission trips. A few years later, Violet did the same. Only now that his brother had a family, Mason would keep to shorter trips. Jake couldn't blame him. If Addy were in his life, he wouldn't want to be away from her for very long, either.

"Then we'll have to pray your first cookbook is a huge success," Lila said with a smile.

"It will be," Finn declared with the utmost confidence. "Aunt Addy lets me taste her recipes. Yummy," he said, sitting back to rub his tummy.

"I second that," Jake agreed, rubbing his, too, eliciting a snort of laughter from his nephew. He looked to Addy. "My only regret is that you won't be here for me to test your recipes for that second cookbook." Wouldn't be a daily part of his life, something he'd come to look forward to. Oh, and how he would miss the warmth of her smile.

"I'm not even sure there will be one," Addy told him. "If the first cookbook doesn't get off the ground, there probably won't be a second one."

Jake helped himself to another biscuit. "Your cookbook is not only going to get off the ground, it's going to be flying off the shelves." He'd make sure of it. Because Addy deserved to have both success and happiness in her life.

"Hey, Vi," Jake said as he rolled into the kitchen, where his sister was working on a flower arrangement she'd brought home from The Flower Shack after dinner.

"Jake!" his sister gasped as she glanced up. "What are you doing moving around the house by yourself?"

"Taking back some of my independence," he replied matter-of-factly. "My physical therapist told me I can start using my arm in a limited capacity." He demonstrated by lifting it slowly out to the side.

"Limited," she repeated with a scolding frown as she stood and walked over to push his chair over to the table, where she'd been clipping the stem off a flower. "I'm sure that was meant as in lifting a fork or buttoning your shirt. Not getting yourself around the house in a wheelchair."

Jake laughed as he worked the arm of his injured shoulder back into its sling. "I promise I'm allowed to do a bit more than that. And for your information, I took my time getting my chair to the kitchen. Slow and steady. It's all good."

She shook her head with a defeated sigh. "I think you're more stubborn than Braden. I keep telling him that I don't need his help at The Flower Shack, yet does he listen? No."

"He wouldn't be the Braden we know if he didn't."

"True." She returned to her seat and reached for the flower she'd laid on the table when she'd seen him enter the room. Inserting its neatly trimmed stem into the arrangement on the table in front of her, she said, "Stubborn or not, it makes my heart so happy to see you getting better each passing day. But then I suppose having someone take such good care of you could only have helped the recovery process."

Having Addy by his side made him happy. If only it didn't have to end. At the reminder of what Addy had done for him, he said, "I was hoping I might find Momma in here."

"Nope," his sister replied. "All you got was me. Where's Addy? The two of you are usually together."

"She went to the mall with Lila to offer her opinion. Apparently, brides not only need a wedding dress for their big day, they also need a special dress for the rehearsal dinner, too."

Violet laughed. "Be thankful Mason's getting married first. You'll know all there is to know when you get married someday."

His getting married. He thought of Addy, envisioning her a creation of satin and lace. She would make a beautiful bride someday. His, he wanted to proclaim. But her heart wasn't his. Yet.

"You know," his sister went on, "I've been so busy helping at The Flower Shack that you and I haven't had much time to really talk."

"Uh-oh," he teased. "This sounds serious."

"I suppose it is," she replied. "I just wanted to say how grateful I am for all the TLC Addy's been giving you since the two of you patched things up. She's helped to bring my brother back to me."

He nodded. "I have to believe God brought her back into my life to help heal me. She has been so patient and caring. Even when I didn't deserve it." And he loved her for it. Loved her for everything that made Addy who she was.

"I think you're right," Violet told him with a soft smile. "And coming back has helped to heal her as well. Addy did something that hurt all of us deeply. Offering forgiveness for something like that takes time. And it needs to be done at each person's level of comfort in doing so or not doing so." She picked up a branch of baby's breath and worked it into the assortment of bright flowers. "I'm just thankful you were able to finally forgive Addy, as we had chosen to, because I've never seen you happier than you've been these past few weeks."

He couldn't deny it. Being around Addy did make him happy. Completed him when he hadn't realized a part of him had been missing. She had helped him push away the bad memories of his time in the Republic of Congo—and made him appreciate that, by the grace of God, he had a future to look forward to. One he saw Addy in so clearly. Only time was running out to make her see they were meant to be so much more than friends

"Addy just so happens to be the reason I was looking for Momma."

"She should be back soon," Violet told him as she busied herself with her floral creation. "She ran into town after dinner to meet with Reverend Hutchins at the church."

His brows drew together. "This late?"

"It's only six-thirty," she replied. "Momma wanted to go over some of the specifics for Mason and Lila's rehearsal dinner that's being held in the church hall. At least, that's the reason Momma gave me this time," she said in a strange singsong kind of voice.

Jake looked up, pinning his sister with his gaze. "This time?"

She laughed. "Come on, Jake, you know what I mean."

"No, I don't," he said even as Addy's observations came rushing back to him.

"It's been to discuss church fund-raisers, potluck dinners, decorative changes to the Sunday school rooms. But we all know it's more than that. Momma and the reverend are sweet on each other. They enjoy spending time together. She just isn't ready to tell us yet." He gave an acknowledging nod, Addy having already made him aware that there might be something special happening between his momma and the reverend. She deserved to be happy. So did he. And like his momma, he needed to seize any opportunity he could to hold onto the happiness he'd found with Addy.

"What did you need Momma for?" she asked.

"I wanted to talk to her about setting up a book signing at the market for Addy before she leaves to go back to Atlanta. Once her book is up for sale, of course."

"Of course. What a great idea," his sister said. "That's so sweet of you."

"Mason's not your only brother who has the ability to be sweet."

"I'm home!"

They looked toward the open doorway at the sound of their momma's voice.

"Jake and I are in the kitchen!" Violet called out.

"Hi, honey," she said to Jake and then looked to the bouquet on the table. "It looks beautiful, Violet. You have a real gift for creating floral arrangements."

Violet smiled. "Thanks, Momma. I enjoy making them." She looked to Jake. "Tell her your incredibly sweet idea for helping Addy out."

And so he did.

"I think that's it," Addy said as she set the last of the bags of baking supplies she'd brought with her on the Landerses' kitchen table.

"Once again," Jake said, "I'm sorry I couldn't be of any help."

"You will be," she assured him. "Unless you've changed your mind about being my guinea pig for this recipe."

"Not a chance," he told her. "The offer still stands."

"Good," she replied with a smile. She enjoyed having Jake's help whenever she was cooking or baking. He assisted as well as he could with the limited use of one arm. He never complained about his limitations, just worked around them. She found herself falling more and more for this strong, determined man. "I guess we'll get started."

"Would you mind holding off long enough to take a short ride in the Gator?"

She looked to Jake. "Right now?"

He nodded. "I'd like to take in a little fresh air before we get busy perfecting that final recipe for you. If that's all right."

Of course he would. She should have thought to suggest it. But she'd been so focused on making sure she had everything she needed with her, she hadn't given any thought to the way they had been doing things. On days she came over to stay with him, she would make him breakfast and then they would go for a ride in Jake's ATV around the orchard, to Mama Tully's and out to the new house Lila and Mason were building. She loved those long rides, taking in the beauty of the world around them, sharing laughter and conversation. But, more importantly, she loved doing something that made Jake happy. Just as his helping her with her recipes brought her so much joy.

"I wouldn't mind a little fresh air," she agreed. "It always helps to free up my creative cooking juices. Just give me a sec to put a few of the ingredients away in the fridge before we go."

Jake watched her, a wide grin on his face.

"What are you up to?" Addy asked as she closed the refrigerator door.

"Me? Up to something?"

She rolled her eyes. "Oh, please. How about we leave the sweet, little innocent boy act as a resource for Finn to use?"

Jake tossed his head back with a chuckle. "Okay, so I'm not so good at trying to hide the fact that I have a secret. But I do intend to hold it long enough for us to take the Gator out for a ride."

A secret? "Good or bad?"

"All good," he assured her.

"Then what are we waiting for?" she asked excitedly as she hurried over to where he sat in his chair.

Five minutes later, they were in the ATV and heading off into the orchard.

"Where to?" she asked.

"Head north toward the pond," he instructed.

She knew the spot well. She had gone fishing there with Mason and Lila during their summer breaks from school. Jake and Violet had joined in a few of those times. She smiled, recalling the little boy Jake had been. Lanky and full of unrestrainable, youthful energy. Big brown eyes and short, wavy brown hair. And a smile that never stopped.

"Don't we need poles to fish?" she teased.

"We would," he agreed, "*if* we were going fishing." Then he looked her way. "Would you like to?"

"It's been years since I held a fishing pole," Addy replied with a smile. "I think I would like to. We always had so much fun at the pond in the summertime."

"Next time we'll bring the rods and give it a go," Jake promised.

And when would that next time be? Once she started working again, she wouldn't be free to pick up and go back to Sweet Springs for a visit as often as she liked. That made her heart ache. Her life in Atlanta was going to feel so empty without Jake in it. She pushed those thoughts away, determined to focus on the time they had together now.

Addy turned onto another path, heading in the direction of the pond. "Lila tells me your momma met with Reverend Hutchins last evening." She glanced his way, awaiting his reaction. Jake nodded. "I know. They were going over plans for Mason and Lila's rehearsal dinner. Violet thinks there's more to it than that."

"I believe I made mention of that the day Reverend Hutchins stopped by the market to pick up one of your momma's pies."

He frowned. "I thought maybe you were misreading the situation. But now I think you might have been right. I'm trying to be happy for her, but it's something I wasn't prepared for."

"So your momma dating would be a problem for you?"

"No. Maybe." He sighed. "She's older than Reverend Hutchins," he said, as if the fact needed pointing out.

"That again," she said with a roll of her eyes.

"Several years older," he attempted to explain. "Not just a few, like you and I."

So their age difference truly wasn't an issue for Jake? Addy felt a surge of hope. Because she had long ago stopped thinking of him as that little boy she'd known. "Jake, they're both adults," she countered. "And while I don't know the reverend's exact age, I doubt there's more than four or five years' difference between them." Addy did her best to hide her hurt at Jake's opinion of a man showing interest in a woman who was older than him. At least she knew where he stood on the matter, despite his saying otherwise.

Jake sighed. "It's not even that as much as it is Momma's having kept it from us if there is something sparking between her and the reverend."

That definitely eased the sting a bit. "Did you ever stop to think that maybe your momma hasn't accepted the depth of her feelings for Reverend Hutchins? Maybe she's afraid to love again. Maybe she's afraid of how her doing so might affect her children. Especially you."

"Why me?" he said indignantly.

"Because you've had enough to deal with in your life recently," Addy explained as best she could, trying to put herself in Mrs. Landers's place. "I can promise you this. Your momma's heart is big. There's more than enough love inside it to share if that's what she chooses to do. And if she does, you have to know that it wouldn't lessen the love she feels for you and Mason and Violet."

He frowned. "I don't want her to get hurt."

"And you think the reverend will hurt her?"

"No," he admitted with a sigh. "Reverend Hutchins is a good man."

"If you truly believe that in your heart, then you should thank the Lord for giving your momma another chance to have that special kind of happiness again, *if* that's what this thing is with the reverend." Addy told him. "We don't always get second chances in life." But she had with Jake. Only she wanted more than a rekindled friendship. She wanted his heart.

"You really have a way with putting things in perspective," he told her with a gentle smile. "Are you sure you don't want to reconsider your career choice and go back to school to be a psychologist?"

"I can't see myself ever wanting to step away from baking," she told him, meaning it. It was a passion that ran deep for her. "But I could combine the two," she added with a grin. "I could create my own version of a fortune cookie, filling them with printed slips of paper offering helpful advice. Like Be Kind to Others, or It's Never Too Late to Say You're Sorry." That last one, especially, hit home for her.

"How about Sometimes You Just Have to Follow Your Heart?" Jake suggested, sounding so serious Addy had to force herself to remember that he was only offering cookie advice ideas. Nothing more.

Following her heart was something she couldn't do. Not right now. Maybe ever. She had only just gotten Jake's friendship back. To ask for more could cost her the comfortable ease between them if Jake didn't reciprocate her feelings.

"Addy," Jake said, drawing her from her thoughts, "you missed the turn."

"What?" Glancing back, she saw the opening in the pines that lined that section of the orchard, beyond which was the pond. "Oops." She turned the ATV around and then drove through the gap in the pines. "It's been a while since I was back here."

"Go ahead and pull up closer to the pond's edge," Jake instructed. "I'd like to be close enough to see into the water."

She laughed. "Boy, you really are a trusting soul."

"I have faith in your driving ability," he replied. "Faith in you."

Her heart melted at those words. Tears threatened to blur her vision. "That means a lot," she told him. "And I feel the same way about you." She eased the ATV up as close to the water's edge as she felt safe doing and then cut the engine. "It looks so different here," she said, glancing around.

"It's been a few years since you've seen it," he agreed. "Trees are a lot bigger. And the grass around the pond isn't quite as beat down as it used to be when we used to fish here as kids."

"It's still such a serene place," she said with a contented sigh. "And the view is so beautiful. I'm so glad you thought to come out here." It was only then she recalled his reason for taking a ride. Addy turned to find Jake watching her.

"Definitely beautiful," he said.

"Um, the view is out there," she said, her arm doing a broad sweep of the pond.

"Not the best view," he countered with a grin.

Her heart gave a little flutter. "When did you become such a sweet-talking flirt?" It was so hard not to be led astray by his playful teasing.

"Just speaking the truth," he told her. "If that's flirting, so be it."

They teased each other often, but this was different. More exciting. It made her feel surprisingly off-balance. "Are you attempting to distract me from our reason for coming here?" Because if he was, he was doing a great job of it.

"Ah, you're referring to the secret I promised to share with you."

"Yes," she said impatiently. "So stop with

the flattery and tell me whatever it is." She added with a smile, "Please."

He leaned back against the seat, tucking his arms casually behind his head. "Well, I've been thinking a lot about your cookbook lately. I know how much this project means to you and wanted to do something to help make it a success."

"Jake, you don't have to—"

"I want to," he said. "That's why I suggested to Momma and the rest of the family that we carry copies to sell at the market. Everyone agreed."

"That's so sweet," she said, deeply touched. To think that Jake put so much effort into supporting her dream. It showed how far they'd come. How much he cared.

He grinned. "It gets sweeter. We'd like to hold a signing for you at the market before you head back to Atlanta. Of course, that depends on whether or not you can get print versions delivered here in time."

Tears sprang to Addy's eyes. What better place to launch her cookbook than in the very place where she'd first discovered her love of baking—his family's peach market! Turning to Jake, Addy threw her arms around him in a grateful hug and then froze, quickly easing her embrace. "Your shoulder," she worried.

"Is much better," he assured her. "Feel free to hug away."

She lifted her gaze to his, and in that moment something shifted between them. And then Jake was kissing her. Or maybe she had kissed him. However it had happened, it felt like she had waited a lifetime for this moment.

When they eased apart, they both sat in stunned silence, their gazes locked.

"I'm sorry," Addy said, feeling the need to apologize. She had allowed her feelings for Jake to carry her away. What if she crossed a line she shouldn't have crossed?

"Don't be," Jake told her with a tender smile. "As far as I'm concerned, that kiss was long overdue."

Addy had never felt so giddy in her life. The sweet and completely unexpected kiss that they'd just shared, followed by Jake's admission that he'd been wanting it, had butterflies fluttering about wildly in her stomach. The feelings she'd been tamping down where Jake was concerned joyously pushed their way to the surface of her heart. There were so many reasons for her to put an end to this shift that was happening in their friendship, but Addy couldn't bring herself to point them out. Instead, she said, "I agree."

Chapter Eleven

Jake had been sitting out on the front porch for close to an hour, soaking up the sunshine and thinking about the kiss he'd shared with Addy by the pond days earlier. The fact that she'd eagerly returned his embrace told him she was finally seeing him as the man he'd become, rather than the boy she'd known. Finally. He'd waited years for that revelation to occur to her. To move beyond just friendship with Addy.

He'd spent the past several days mulling over their situation and trying to come up with a way to make a relationship work for them…if Addy were willing to give things a try. Keeping her happiness in mind, he'd come up with a plan. If only he could keep the doubt that seemed determined to creep into his thoughts at bay. Like what if he'd only imagined Addy's response to his kiss? Maybe she had just accepted it to keep from causing him the embarrassment of her rejection. Then he'd recall the brief glances she'd cast in his direction when she thought he wasn't paying attention. The blush that spread across her cheeks when their gaze would meet, and the smile that always followed, made him more determined than ever to win Addy's heart completely.

A car coming up the road pulled Jake from his musings. He looked to see Reverend Hutchins pulling up to the market. No doubt to pick up his weekly pie. The reverend waved in greeting as he stepped from his car.

"Afternoon, Reverend," Jake called out, returning the wave.

The preacher cast a brief glance toward the market before turning and heading across the yard to where Jake sat watching him from his wheelchair.

This was the man who had found a place in his momma's heart. One that had only been held by his daddy for more years than Jake had been alive. But he felt no resentment toward the man. Reverend Hutchins had made her smile again. He just prayed the reverend's intentions were the same as his momma's.

"It's good to see you out enjoying the day."

"Winter will be here before we know it," Jake replied. They were already into November. "No sense wasting a day like this by sitting inside."

Reverend Hutchins nodded. "Agreed. How are you feeling? You look well."

"I'm getting there," Jake replied. "Patience has been a hard-to-grasp virtue through all this. Lots of prayers sent up." At least there had been since he'd stopped blaming God for Corey's death and had returned to church. The support he'd received there had made him grateful to be a part of the faith community.

"Understandably so," Reverend Hutchins said. "The body heals at its own pace. I know I told you how sorry I was after you came home from that trip, but I'd like to say it again. Ever since our church received word about the attack, I've been filled with so much guilt."

Jake hadn't expected that. "Why? You had nothing to do with the shooting."

"I approved your going on that trip to the Republic of Congo to help build the new schoolhouse. There were other mission trips, safer destinations, that I could have agreed to have our program be a part of," the reverend explained. "You have no idea how many talks I've had with the Lord, trying to ease my conscience."

"I knew where I was going," Jake said. "Knew the risks. Don't suffer any more guilt on my behalf," he told the reverend.

"I'll try my best," the older man replied. "What I need to do is focus more on how blessed we were that there weren't more lives lost that day."

Jake nodded, thinking of Corey. It wasn't nearly as painful as it had been to think of his friend. Opening up to Addy about that loss had served as a balm to the festering wound Corey's death had left in his gut. "I've been trying to do the same." He met the reverend's gaze. "Momma doesn't know anyone was killed in the ambush that day, does she?" Had that been something they'd discussed during their get-togethers? She'd never made mention of it to him if they had.

The reverend shook his head. "If you had wanted to share the details of that day with her, you would have. It wasn't my place to do so."

"I appreciate that, Reverend. Momma was upset enough as it was when she'd learned I'd been injured. I didn't see any reason to upset her further."

He glanced toward the market and then

back to Jake. "I think it was the right thing to do. I also know that if your momma had lost you that day, I'm not sure she could have ever recovered from it. You children are her heart."

"You seem to know her pretty well," Jake said.

"We're very good friends," the reverend answered with a nod.

"How good?"

The reverend blinked. "Excuse me?"

"I may be way off base here, but I've always felt that I could be open with you."

"You can," the older man replied. "And I'll answer that honestly. I think your momma is the kindest, most giving woman I know. I admire her strength and dedication to her family and to God. I can sympathize with what she went through after losing your daddy. I lost my wife the year before I took over at the Sweet Springs church. Your momma and I have had many talks over the years, sharing our feelings of grief over the loss of our spouses, and from that a special friendship has grown between us."

"I'm sorry for your loss. I had no idea," Jake told him. He'd just assumed the reverend had never married. "I'm glad Momma had you to talk to." Just as he'd shared his deepest pain with Addy. Everyone needed someone they could open themselves up to—good or bad. "I'll be honest, too. I think Momma feels more than friendship toward you."

His face lit up, telling Jake the depth of the reverend's feelings toward his momma. "You do?"

"She's never actually said anything," Jake hurried to clarify, not wanting to give false hope. "It's just a feeling Mason, Violet and I all have. I'm only telling you this because I don't want to see Momma get hurt."

The reverend offered a kind smile. "Neither do I. Nor had I wanted to assume my feelings were reciprocated, which is why I've never pushed for more than friendship from her. Because I'd rather have our friendship than risk having nothing at all."

That was how Jake had felt about Addy, until he'd come to realize that the risk was worth taking. And that's what he'd been doing. Showing Addy in any way he could how he felt about her. Helping her with her cookbook, showering her with compliments, and letting her know how much he enjoyed spending time with her. "Again, it's not my business," he said, "but I think you should consider taking that risk and letting Momma know how you feel." Just as he intended to do with Addy, because everyone deserved the chance to have true happiness in their life.

The reverend looked surprised. "And you and Mason and Violet would be all right with that?"

"We would," Jake told him. "We talked it over among ourselves and all agreed that should something start up between you and Momma, we'd be happy for you both. I can't think of a better man for her to have in her life."

A sheen of moisture filled the reverend's eyes. Clearing the emotion from his throat, he said, "That means a lot, Jake. Thank you." Holding out his hand, he said, "I think it's time for me to let your momma know where my feelings lie."

Jake took the offered hand. "Something tells me we'll be needing to set one more place at our table for our Sunday dinners." Two more if things worked out with Addy the way he hoped they would. Because he was about to follow the advice he'd given the reverend and take a heart risk of his own.

"Jake!" Addy said with a gasp of surprise as she stepped from her car. "Where's your wheelchair?"

"Back at the house," he replied with a smile.

"I came over to let Momma know we were heading into town."

"Where did those come from?" she asked, worriedly eyeing the crutches braced under his arms. "Should you even be up on your feet? And what about your shoulder?"

He chuckled. "I picked them up on my way home from therapy the other day. Right after I received the all-clear from my therapist to get them. My shoulder is good. The leg still has a way to go, but at least I'll be able to get around without having to rely on everyone pushing me from this place to that in a wheelchair."

"I didn't mind," she told him.

"I know you didn't," he said with a warm smile. "And you have no idea how much I appreciate all you've done for me."

His smile started a swirl of butterflies in her stomach. "Why didn't you say something?"

"I wanted to surprise you."

"You definitely did that," she said, forgetting just how tall he was. However, bent over as he was to use his crutches, brought his face much closer to hers. It made Addy remember the special moment they had shared. Had her wishing he would kiss her again.

"I have a surprise, too," Addy said, barely able to contain her excitement.

"Must be something really good," he noted, "if that smile you're wearing is any indication. Would it happen to have anything to do with your cookbook?"

"Yes," she blurted out. "It's done! Uploaded and set to go up for sale in one week! At least the digital version will be. The print version will take a few days longer to be available for order."

A wide grin split his face. "Addy, that's wonderful news! If I weren't still learning to master these crutches, I'd be giving you the biggest bear hug right now. What do you say I treat you to a celebratory dinner while we're in town?"

"I'd like that." She wouldn't have minded being pulled into his embrace either. But dinner would be wonderful as well. There was no one she wanted to celebrate with more. Jake had been there for her more than she could have ever hoped for. Smiling happily, she walked alongside Jake as they made their way out to her car, making sure to keep enough distance between them that she wouldn't accidentally bump his crutch.

"So what's next?" he asked. "Now that your book's ready to go."

"There's so much to do now," she said as she moved to open the passenger door for him. "I'll need to order bookmarks, set up some sort of online promotion to get the word out and order some print copies for sending out to reviewers."

"Wow," he said as he lowered himself carefully into the car. "That's a lot. I'd offer to help, but I know nothing about that side of publishing. I'll have to stick to taste testing recipes for you," he said with a grin.

"I didn't know much about it either," she admitted as she carefully fed the crutches into the back seat. "Thankfully, there's a ton of info out there on the internet to guide me in the right direction."

Addy hurried around to the driver's side and slid in behind the wheel. "Talk about a day filled with surprises."

"With more to come," Jake muttered as they pulled away from the house.

"More?" Addy replied with a glance in his direction. Jake was looking out the window, a wide grin spilling across his face. What was he up to now? It made her think back to the first time she'd seen him after her return. He had looked at her with such an icy gaze that she had shuddered inwardly. They had come so far. She had learned just how precious a smile could be. Jake's, in particular.

"I can hear your thoughts churning," Jake

said, looking her way. "You might as well give them a rest. A surprise is a surprise. That means I'm not going to tell you what it is ahead of time."

She laughed. "Easier said than done."

True to his word, Jake kept his secret locked up tight the whole way into town. He had her pull into an empty parking space between the hardware store and the beauty shop. Braden was waiting for them in front of a vacant storefront that sat between the two other businesses.

Jake didn't wait for Addy's help. He was already up, balancing on one foot as he secured his crutches under his arms. "You got it?" he asked Braden.

His best friend nodded. "Got it." Pushing away from the wall, he started toward them.

Got what? Braden's hands were empty. Addy looked to Jake questioningly.

"Those wheels," he said, grinning.

"Afternoon, Addy," Braden said when he reached them.

"Afternoon," she replied and then watched as Braden pulled something from his pocket and handed it over to Jake.

"Appreciate it," Jake told him.

"Any time," Braden replied. "New transportation, I see," he said, nodding toward the crutches.

Jake nodded. "I'm getting there."

"Well," Braden said, looking Addy's way. "I'd best let the two of you get to that surprise Jake has for you." With a wave, he headed off down the sidewalk in the direction of the flower shop.

Addy turned to Jake. "Braden knows what the secret is?"

"Had to tell him," Jake explained. "I needed his help with this one. Are you ready for your surprise?"

"Do you even have to ask?" she said excitedly, ready to follow him wherever.

Only Jake didn't go anywhere. He worked himself around on his crutches until he was facing the vacant storefront.

"Jake," she said, laughing at his silliness. "What are you doing?"

He produced a key and inserted it into the door's lock. "Giving you another option for a career path." Pushing the door open, he motioned her inside.

"I don't understand," she said as she stepped past him. "What does this have to do with my being a pastry chef?"

"Everything, if you want it to," he replied as he joined her, balancing himself on his crutches as he closed the door behind him. Sunlight streamed in through the nearly floor-to-ceiling picture windows and filled the room with light. "This place is about to go on the market. I was thinking about buying it and leasing it out for a really low rate—to you."

"To me?"

"Addy, I've never seen you happier than when you're baking and creating your own recipes." He motioned to the room around him. "It wouldn't take much to make this place your own. The town doesn't have a pastry shop or a bakery. Why not do what you love in the town that you love?"

Shock filled her. "Jake," she said in a soft gasp. She was so touched by his generous offer. To think that he was willing to buy a building for the sole purpose of giving her a place to start her own business. Oh, how she loved this kind, giving man.

"Addy, please hear me out before you say anything," he said with a gentle smile. "You're between jobs. This is your chance to do something you have a true passion for while giving the town something it doesn't have. I know you were concerned about funds when we talked about your going into business on your own before. I've got money to invest in the building. I can see to any updates to the apartment upstairs and rent it out to help cover the cost of the mortgage. You could fix this bottom floor up however you like," he said, looking around. "Create the bakery you've envisioned in your dreams."

Jake's barely restrained excitement spilled over to her. *My own bakery.* How many times had she dreamed about that very thing? Addy let the possibility sink in for a long moment as her gaze drifted about the empty room. The building was older, but the current owner had seen to its upkeep well enough. She could tell it had been vacant for several months or more, because several small gossamer webs stretched from ceiling to wall in two of the corners, shimmering in the sunlight. A light layer of dust coated the hardwood floors. That didn't keep Addy from pushing those things aside in her mind and imagining the changes she would make to the place if it were hers to do with what she would.

She envisioned the walls painted in warm, soothing pastel shades. Long, glass-front display cases filled with an assortment of that day's selections. Each of the storefront window shelves decorated specially for each month or holiday with hunger-tempting displays meant to draw in passersby.

"Can you see it, Addy?" Jake asked. "A

bakery specializing in all those sweet treats you so love to bake. *Your* bakery."

"Yes," she said with a sigh. It was a dream so close she could almost touch it. The time spent in Sweet Springs with Jake had shown her that home really was where the heart was. This was her home. A place she would love to be a part of, start a business in, continue building her relationship with Jake. For him to have gone to these lengths, he had to feel something more than friendship for her. Didn't he?

"I don't want to push you," he said, reining in a bit of his enthusiasm, "just give you another option. A place where you could be your own boss, choose your own recipes to make, set vacation days whenever you wanted them."

Addy laughed softly. "No pushing there."

"Okay, consider it a small nudge. But only if this is what you want," he added.

He was giving her an option she hadn't thought a possibility. And Jake would be a fair and honest landlord, she knew. It would be a good business opportunity for Jake, too. That made her feel less guilty about actually considering what he was so generously offering her.

She turned to look up at Jake, her heart

catching in her throat. "You are the kindest, most giving man I've ever known." A man so worth loving, and love him she did.

He smiled warmly. "I enjoy spending time with you, something I won't be able to do if you're back in Atlanta. So part of my offer is definitely on the selfish side. And then there's the people in Sweet Springs and the surrounding counties who will, no doubt, be thrilled to have a local bakery with the quality of baked goods I know you could offer them. But it's your happiness with whatever career path you choose to travel in your life that matters most."

Tears flooded her eyes. "Jake," she groaned.

"I didn't mean to make you cry, Addy girl," he replied with so much tenderness in his voice that several tears fell free, sliding down her cheeks.

Addy girl. That endearment made her feel like she was his. Like his world was hers. Like there truly was a chance for her to have it all, Jake included.

"Addy," he sighed, a fretful expression on his handsome face.

"I'm okay," she said with a sniffle. Gathering up a smile, she looked up into his eyes. "Thank you, Jake. For everything. For the laughter. For your help with my recipes. For supporting my dreams. For forgiving me."

Jake reached out to gently brush away the stray tears with the pad of his thumb. "You left something out."

She looked up at him questioningly.

Propping a crutch against the wall beside him, Jake used his free arm to draw her closer. "For loving you." He lowered his head, pressing his lips to hers in a sweet kiss.

Jake loved her. Addy's heart melted into one big sugary-sweet puddle of happiness, but at the same time fear urged her to take a step back. She knew better than most that love wasn't always enough. Her momma loved her, yet life had been complicated for them, and so unpredictable. And when she'd been taken into foster care, Addy had learned that lesson. Could she trust in her love for Jake, his love for her, long enough to give them a chance to find a way to make things work?

Jake offered up a gentle smile. "Those mental wheels are turning again, I see."

She looked up into his tender gaze, returning his smile. "I'm not sure they ever stop. Jake…" she said, tearing up again.

"You don't have to say anything," he told her. "I just needed you to know where my heart lies. I don't want there to be any more secrets between us ever again. Even if friendship is all you're able to—"

She pressed a finger to his lips. "Shh… I have something I need to say." She let her hand fall away.

He stood there, waiting patiently, a hint of something akin to yearning in those dark eyes.

She could see the love there. Could feel it wrap its invisible arms around her. Her smile softened. "I love you, too. And while starting my own bakery wasn't really a consideration for me when I left Atlanta for Sweet Springs, I will definitely add it to my options."

She loves me!

Jake wanted to pick her up and swing her around, but his injuries kept him from seeing that urge through. "I pray this isn't some dream I'm about to wake up from."

"I feel the same way," Addy replied. "Are you sure the age difference isn't going to be an issue for you? I saw how you reacted to the thought of your momma being interested in someone younger than her."

He shook his head. "Your being older than me never made a difference for me. I was just waiting for you to realize that I'm more than Mason's little brother. As for Momma, I admit that did throw me off a bit at first. But think-ing of one's momma dating anyone takes a few extra chews to swallow, younger man or not. Reverend or not. But I could never be-grudge Momma the same happiness that I've found with you."

"I'm so glad you feel that way. I know it wasn't easy for you to process at first. Your parents were happily married for so many years. My momma never had that until Ben came along, so it was something I never had to experience."

"I'm glad your momma found someone."

She smiled up at him. "Me, too."

"Finding that special someone made me realize how lonely Momma must have been since Daddy passed," he said with a tender smile. "Once I'd taken a little time to mull things over, I knew I needed to talk to Rev-erend Hutchins. The opportunity presented itself the other day when he stopped by the market and saw me sitting on the porch. He came over to say hello, and we talked."

Her eyes widened. "You did?"

He nodded.

"What did you say to him?"

"I told him that I don't want to see Momma invest her heart in someone who isn't able to reciprocate those feelings for one reason or another. The reverend made it crystal clear where his intentions lay. I, in turn, told him he has my blessing to see where things might go with Momma. Mason and Violet's, too, because the three of us have been discussing our feelings, and we'd be happy to have him become a special part of our momma's life."

"And…?" she prompted.

"If he has his way, he and Momma will be enjoying meals out for more than their need to discuss church issues."

"I knew it," Addy said, her face lighting up.

"I guess this is where you get to say I told you so," he teased with a grin.

Addy pretended to zip her lips.

Jake released a husky chuckle. "I appreciate your declining to point out my habit of wearing blinders when it came to Momma and Reverend Hutchins's budding relationship."

"Better late than never."

"That goes for us as well." He had nearly thrown this chance away over his refusal to forgive her. He was so grateful for her persistence. It had made him realize what truly mattered. *Who* truly mattered. Addy was the woman he wanted to spend the rest of his life with, be it in Sweet Springs or Atlanta. They could find a way to make things work. "Now, enough about Momma's happiness. Time to get back to yours. I still haven't shown you the back room, where you could have a kitchen put in if you decide to accept my offer. Or the upstairs apartment, which I would have renovated before renting it out if I end up buying this place." It was then he noted she was no longer smiling.

A worried frown creased her slender brows.

"Something wrong?" he asked.

"You're still recovering from your injuries," she pointed out, her gaze zeroing in on the crutches at his sides. "I don't think it's a very good idea for you to be escorting me all over this old building. Or renovating buildings."

"If it will make you feel better, I'll wait here while you take a peek around."

She nodded. "Okay."

"And as far as renovations go, I'll contract out the work I can't do physically right now."

She nodded, relief clear on her face. "Stay here while I go take a peek," she told him. "I won't be long."

"Take your time," Jake called after her as she walked away. He wanted her to really be able to envision the place as the bakery she'd only ever dreamed of owning. Just as he'd begun envisioning the kind of life he'd never thought he could have with Addy. He just prayed they settled down and raised a family in Sweet Springs. Because there they would be surrounded by so many who loved them. A place where Addy had mentioned more than once she was happiest.

Chapter Twelve

Several days had passed since Jake had made his very generous offer. An offer Addy hadn't been able to push from her thoughts. The possibility excited her as much as it terrified her. What if she invested money into a bakery of her own and it didn't end up a success? If that happened, she could find herself struggling to make ends meet. These concerns were why she'd spent time doing research and speaking to other area bakeries. There was a clear need for one in Sweet Springs, and the traffic passing through town on a daily basis supported the already existing stores. A positive sign for her future business there if she decided to accept Jake's generous offer.

Even so, memories of her childhood were determined to spill over into the present. Despite knowing that she wouldn't go hungry if her business failed, she struggled to set them aside. If she chose this new career path, she would need to invest in equipment and supplies for her bakery. That meant having less of a cushion in her bank account to lean on.

Just knowing she would have Jake there, supporting her in her endeavor, believing in her, made the risk so much more worth considering. But she wanted more than his shoulder to lean on. She wanted his heart forever. Wanted a family. But what kind of mother would she be? Her upbringing had been far from the norm. Could she be the kind of parent Jake's future children deserved? Catching herself, Addy put on the mental brakes. Jake had said he loved her. But he'd never spoken about marriage or starting a family.

The ringing of her cell phone pulled Addy from her warring thoughts. Setting her hairbrush down, she reached for the cell phone lying on the dresser in front of her. A glance at the screen showed a number she didn't recognize. Answering the call, she brought the phone to her ear. "Hello?"

"Ms. Mitchell? Adeline Mitchell?" a woman asked on the other end of the line.

"This is she," she replied.

"Good afternoon. This is Chantel Wilks with Greenford Country Club. I'm calling in regard to the job application we received from you a few weeks back. We've recently had an unexpected opening for our head pastry chef position, and I recalled seeing your résumé come through. You are more than qualified for the job, and the references you listed gave you glowing reviews. Have you accepted a position elsewhere yet?"

"No," Addy said, shaking her head. "I haven't."

"Well, if you're still interested, I'd like to offer you the position," Ms. Wilks said and then proceeded to go over the offer package they were extending to her for their head pastry chef position. A very generous offer. Months earlier she would have been ecstatic over this opportunity. It was the direction she'd planned to go in after being let go from her previous job. But everything had changed for her since coming back to Sweet Springs. She now had Jake's offer to consider when making her decision.

"I'm out of town at the moment but will be returning to Atlanta in a week. How soon would you be needing an answer?" Addy asked.

"We had hoped to bring someone in immediately, but we also want the right person.

Take a few days to decide. In the meantime, I will email you all the pertinent information."

"Thank you," Addy said appreciatively. "I'll look it over and will get back to you soon."

When the call ended, Addy set her phone down and then reached for the discarded hairbrush in a daze. This was what she'd wanted. To find a job as a head pastry chef. And while it wasn't a hotel, she would be working for the very prestigious Greenford Country Club. More people working under her. More money than she'd been making before. So why didn't that make her heart happy?

Addy knew the answer to that question. It was because of all she stood to lose if she were to accept the offer. The chance to own her own business. The chance to live in Sweet Springs—the one place where she was the happiest. And she could risk losing Jake, right when they had finally moved past a friendship and had started an actual relationship, if she accepted the job offer at the country club. Long-distance relationships were hard for so many reasons. Not that she wouldn't do everything she could to make things work between them once she returned to Atlanta. *If* she chose to return to a life there.

"The package guy was here!" Finn called

out from what Addy concluded was the front porch.

Her cookbooks! Tossing the brush onto her bed, she hurried from the room.

Lila shot out of the living room, nearly colliding with Addy as they both raced for the front door.

Laughing, Addy grabbed onto Lila in an attempt to steady them both. "Sorry."

"My fault," Lila said apologetically. "Perfect example of why Mama Tully used to tell us not to run in the house."

Addy nodded as they walked together at a much slower pace to the open front door.

"I was hoping it might be those little plastic umbrellas you fill with mints that I ordered to set out beside the guest book at the reception," Lila explained as she pushed open the screen door.

"I thought it might be my cookbooks," Addy said as she followed her out. Although there was a far greater chance of it being Lila's package. Items for her and Mason's wedding had been arriving almost daily for the past few weeks.

"It's for Aunt Addy," Finn announced, waving them over.

Addy suddenly felt like a kid on Christmas morning. At least, like she had during those few holidays she'd spent in Sweet Springs with Mama Tully.

"It's a real big box," Finn said as he eyed the package.

"That's because there are a whole lot of cookbooks inside it," Addy explained.

"Ooh!" Lila said with a squeal. "I can't wait to see them!"

"What's all the commotion?" Mama Tully asked as she came around the side of the house, where she had been tending to her garden.

"Aunt Addy's cookbooks are here!" Finn said excitedly, pointing to the shipping box near the door.

Mama Tully's face lit up. "They are?"

Addy nodded with a grin, barely able to contain her excitement.

"Well, what's everyone standing around for?" Mama Tully asked. "Let's get this box inside so you can open it."

"You don't have to tell me twice," Addy said, eager to see her creation all put together. But when she bent to lift it, the weight surprised her. "Oh, wow. It's heavy."

"Here," Lila said, stepping around to the other side of the package, "let me help." She bent to test the box's weight. "Are you sure they didn't send you a box of bricks instead?"

"Need a hand?"

They turned to see Mason crossing the front yard to the porch.

"Talk about perfect timing," Lila said, greeting her fiancé with a warm, welcoming smile. "But be forewarned. This package weighs a ton."

"I'm pretty sure I can handle it. I lift baskets and crates filled with peaches for a living," he replied, his attention fixed on Lila as he came up onto the porch.

The tender looks exchanged between her sister and her heart's match were filled with so much love that Addy's thoughts shifted to the man who made her feel the very same way. Jake.

"One of Addy's dreams finally coming true," Lila said as she followed Mason and Finn inside.

"I can't wait to see your cookbook," Mama Tully said as Addy grabbed for the closing screen door, holding it open for her foster mother.

"You and me both." Addy stood in the doorway, watching them go. It was there, in that box that Mason carried with him. Her dream. After years of wanting to create one, after months and months of perfecting recipes and putting them all together, her cookbook had finally become a reality. But the one person who should be there with her for the unveiling wasn't.

"Hurry up, Aunt Addy!" Finn called out from the living room.

She stepped inside, easing the screen door closed behind her. However, instead of joining them, she went straight to her room to grab her purse.

"Addy?" Lila called out.

Addy stepped from her room, meeting her friend halfway down the hallway. "I can't open it without Jake being here," she told her as she pulled her car keys from her purse.

Lila nodded with an understanding smile. "Of course you can't. I'll let everyone know. We'll see you when you get back."

"I won't be long," Addy told her and then hurried past her and out the front door.

"Knock, knock!"

Jake looked up from the peanut butter and jelly sandwich he was making, a smile stretching across his face at those familiar words. Whenever Addy came over, she would open the front door and call out.

"I'm in the kitchen!" he called back with a grin.

A second later, Addy came into the room

in more of a rush than he'd ever seen her do before.

He immediately stopped what he was doing. "What's wrong?" he asked with a worried frown.

"Nothing's wrong," she assured him with a soft smile. "In fact, everything is perfect. My cookbooks came today."

"They did?" he replied. "That's wonderful. How did it feel to hold your cookbook in your hands for the very first time?"

"I'll let you know in a few minutes," she replied with a smile. "After you come back to Mama Tully's with me. I told Lila I wasn't going to open the box without you there with me."

"Addy," he said, emotion tugging at his voice. To know that she'd put off seeing her long-awaited cookbook until he could be there with her for its reveal was an honor that touched him deeply.

"Jake, you were such a big part of making that dream come true. I didn't want to see my cookbook for the first time without you." Glancing down at his partially made lunch, she said, "I'll call and let Lila know we'll be back after you finish with your lunch."

"Lunch can wait," he said. Grabbing for the lids to the peanut butter and jelly, he screwed both tops back on as quickly as he could. "Seeing your cookbook can't."

"Jake, please don't skip lunch on my account."

"I won't be," he replied. "After we see your cookbook, I'd like to take you to lunch to celebrate. Actually," he said with a glance down at his casted leg, "you would have to get us there, but I'll be paying for our meals."

"I'd like that," she said, the corners of her mouth lifting even higher.

Reaching for his crutches, he got to his feet. "Let's go."

They made their way out to her car. Once she had Jake settled in the passenger seat, crutches stored in the back seat, Addy drove them back to Mama Tully's.

"I'm so proud of you," Jake said, his heart overflowing with love for her. And this was only the beginning of her endeavors. He had faith that her first collection of recipes would be a tremendous success. One that would beg for others to follow.

She glanced his way with a bright smile. "I'm sort of proud of me, too."

She should be. She'd come such a long way from that lost little girl who had no dreams to reach for. "Love you, Addy."

Her eyes misted over. "Love you back."

Moments later, they were pulling up to Mama Tully's place. Lila, Finn, Mama Tully and Mason were all standing out on the front porch, waving bright red balloons in the air above their heads.

Addy stepped from her car, laughing. "Balloons?"

"This is a celebration," Lila announced.

Mason reached over to give Finn's hair a playful tousle. "They were my son's idea."

"Nice touch," Jake said with a grin as he made his way alongside Addy to the porch.

"Come on in, you two," Mama Tully said with a wave of her balloon. "I'm ready to see my girl's cookbook."

Jake felt the same way. And he couldn't wait to see the joy on "his girl's" face the moment she laid eyes on her book. The first of many, if things went as well as he had a gut feeling they would.

Mason opened the door, motioning them all inside. They made their way into the living room, where Addy's package sat atop the oak coffee table in the center of the room.

Crutches tucked securely beneath his arms, Jake made his way over to the far side of the room to watch.

"Oh no, you don't," Addy said, pinning him with her gaze. "I need you here with me," she told him and then smiled. "You sacrificed yourself to make sure the recipes I put in my cookbook were at least edible. Therefore, you should share this moment with me."

"It was a daunting task, but somebody had to do it," he replied with a grin as he worked his way back to the coffee table to stand beside her. But he would willingly sacrifice so much more for her. Anything to assure her happiness if it were in his ability to do so. "And I will gladly do the same for your next cookbook."

"Offer accepted," Addy told him before turning that beautiful smile of hers to the box. She carefully peeled away the strip of tape that sealed it shut and then lifted the flaps to reveal the contents inside.

Her gasp had Jake leaning over to peer inside, fearing that something had gone awry.

"They're perfect," she breathed, tears filling her eyes as Addy lifted one of the spiral-bound books from the batch to run her fingers over its cover.

On the front was a picture she had taken on Jake's front porch. She'd draped a lace tablecloth over the wicker table in front of his momma's settee and placed on it two plates filled with her Perfect Peach Cobbler recipe. The dessert had been garnished with blackberries and a dollop of whipped cream. A glass of iced tea with a sprig of mint had been placed next to each plate.

He remembered wanting to gobble it up as he'd sat off to the side watching, but knowing he had to wait until Addy had gotten the perfect shot for its recipe page. What he hadn't known was that she'd chosen that recipe to grace the cover. One she had created in honor of his momma and the time she'd spent teaching Addy all her baking secrets when Addy was living in Sweet Springs.

"Oh, Addy, it's beautiful," Lila sighed.

"I can't see it," Finn complained as he rose up on his toes to peek inside the open box.

Addy reached down and grabbed another cookbook, handing it over to him with a smile. "Here you go."

He looked to his momma. "Now you can make me all the good things Aunt Addy makes for me."

"Me, too," Mason joined in.

Lila looked to Addy, brow lifting.

"Sorry," she said with a giggle.

"That's okay," Lila said. "To be honest, your cookbook will come in handy, when feeding these two sweet-toothed men."

"I'd be happy to bake for you as well," Mason offered.

Jake snorted. "You don't want that. Mason did not inherit any of Momma's cooking abilities."

"You're a fine one to talk," his brother countered.

Mama Tully laughed, shaking her head. "It's a good thing the Lord thought to bestow you two with women who can cook."

Jake nodded in agreement. The Lord had blessed him with a very special woman. One he hoped to make a permanent part of his life.

After the book's unveiling, Mason, Lila and Finn left for the new house, and Mrs. Tully went back out to do some more weeding in her garden.

"I'm glad you came to get me," Jake told Addy as she settled onto the sofa next to him. "I loved seeing your face when you saw your cookbook for the first time. Maybe you'll be creating new recipes for your next one in the kitchen of your very own bakery."

Her smile faded with his suggestion. "About that," she began.

"Addy," he said, trying not to make his tone a pleading one, "what's wrong?"

"I've had a job offer come through. It's a head pastry chef position at a private country club in Atlanta."

It was as if someone had just dumped a

bucket of ice water over his head. Jake felt the future he'd begun to dream of with Addy suddenly slipping away. He wanted to beg her to refuse the offer. To stay there in Sweet Springs with him. But his love for Addy was stronger than his need for his own happiness. He loved her enough to let her go if that's where her career dreams took her. Loved her enough not to try and keep her from achieving her career goals.

"I haven't accepted the job yet," she told him. "I wanted to talk to you first."

The word *yet* effectively deflated the bubble of hope he'd built around Addy's staying in Sweet Springs. Her not giving an answer meant she was considering the offer. But then, he'd known from the start this was a possibility.

"I'm happy for you," he said, though the words tasted like sawdust in his mouth.

"You are?"

For her, yes. For himself in this situation, no. Jake forced a smile. "I know how much your career means to you and how hard it was to have everything you'd worked for over the years taken away. This is a chance for you to have that back again. If that's what you decide to do, I will support you one hundred percent." Even if that meant having to find a way to hold on to what they had from a distance.

Addy put her car in Park and glanced out the driver's side window. Cars filled the lot, even though the signing wasn't scheduled to begin for another half an hour. She could see the gathering crowd milling inside The Perfect Peach through the large front picture windows. A wonderful turnout for her very first book signing. For that alone, she should be ecstatic. But all she could think about was the conversation she'd had with Jake a few days earlier.

If Jake loved her the way he'd said he did, why hadn't he pushed harder for her to stay? Remind her again of his offer to help her open a bakery of her own? Maybe he was having second thoughts about doing so. About her. Whatever his reason, Jake seemed comfortable with the idea of letting her go. The problem was Addy wasn't ready for him to let her go. And she was fully prepared to fight for his love—if only she had more time to do so in person. She was leaving in a few short days to go back to her life in Atlanta, where she would spend Thanksgiving with her momma and stepdaddy. Jake had promised to come visit, but it wouldn't be the same as seeing him every day. And she hated the thought of being so far from those who had become her other family. And Mason and Lila's wedding in the spring suddenly seemed an eternity away.

Grabbing her purse, Addy slung it up over her shoulder and stepped from her car. Her gaze was drawn to the festive lights gracing the front of The Perfect Peach. Despite her troubled thoughts, a calming warmth filled her as she took in the soft glow of the white lights lining the storefront windows and the decorated pine wreath that hung from the entrance door. It was only mid-November but, as she did every year, Jake's momma had succeeded in making it feel like Christmas had arrived early.

Lighted candy canes lit the walkway up to the store's deep-set porch, welcoming Addy inside. She had worried about holding the book signing in the evening, but now she couldn't imagine a better time to have it. It allowed all those who came a chance to enjoy the preholiday decor and set the mood for things to come.

Jake met her at the door. "You've got a full house in here."

Addy nodded. As she scanned the crowded

room, her heartbeat quickened. "I didn't expect this," she admitted.

"I did," he told her with a smile. "Come on," he said, inclining his head. "We're all ready for the town's first author."

"It's a cookbook," she reminded him as he accompanied her over to the festively decorated table she would be using for the book signing. One she hadn't been allowed to see. Lila and Violet had wanted to surprise her and had set everything up the evening prior.

"A book's a book as far as I'm concerned," he told her. "And you put as much time, if not more, into creating yours. You're an author. Believe it, Addy. I do." He motioned to the swarm of people headed in their direction. "So do they."

Emotion knotted in her throat. She was an author.

Finn ran over to greet her. "Aunt Addy! Look at all the people that came for you."

"I see that," she said, finding it hard to speak. She, a girl who had once lived in a car, was now surrounded by so many who truly wished her well in her endeavors.

"And I get to help Momma check them out after you sign their book."

"Then we had better get to work. There are a lot of people here to buy my cookbook."

Nodding excitedly, he moved to stand behind the makeshift checkout table that had been set up near hers.

As Addy took her place behind the neatly stacked cookbooks, her gaze fell on the floral arrangement placed next to them.

"Surprise," Violet said with a bright smile.

"Violet, did you make this?" Addy asked in awe as she eyed the unexpected surprise. The frosted pine arrangement was filled with glittery miniatures of cookies and pie slices, along with a scattering of tiny rolling pins, whisks and wooden spoons, and topped off with a red-and-white-striped bow that had been strategically placed front and center.

She nodded. "I did."

"It's beautiful," Addy told her with a grateful smile. "Thank you so much."

"It was my pleasure," Jake's sister replied. "You know how much I love creating all things floral."

"I'm making a note of that for my and Mason's wedding," Lila interjected with a teasing grin.

Violet looked to her future sister-in-law. "Ask and ye shall receive."

It was then Addy noted that Jake's entire family, Mama Tully, Lila, Finn, Braden and even Reverend Hutchins had all come over to stand in a half circle behind her, offering their support.

"I hope you have enough copies," Lila leaned in to whisper as she passed by on her way to stand next to her son.

"I do, too," Addy called after her. Then she turned to smile in greeting at the first person in line. "Thank you so much for coming. Who would you like me to make this out to?" she asked as she reached for one of several pens lying atop the table in front of her.

Jake thought the line would never end. There was no denying that Addy's cookbook signing had been a huge success. He was happy for her. She deserved this. Every time she'd look over to smile at him, it reminded him of how he wanted to make that smile a permanent part of his life.

So much had changed in his life during the almost two months Addy had been back in Sweet Springs. When she'd first arrived, he'd been bound to a wheelchair as he recovered from his wounds, swallowed up by guilt, and angry at God. Addy, the last person he'd wanted to see, had been the only one capable of pushing life's storm clouds away and giving him a glimpse of the sun. She'd taught him to be grateful for the life he'd been given a second chance at living, that being in a wheelchair didn't have to keep one from finding joy in even the smallest of things. Like a balm to his soul, Addy had helped him to accept that he wasn't to blame for his friend's death, allowing him to make his peace with God.

As the final customers spilled out of the market and everyone else moved about tidying up the store, Jake stepped over to the table where Addy stood gathering up the pens she'd used for her signing. To his surprise, he saw that she held one last cookbook in the crook of her arm. He was so sure she'd signed away the last of her supply minutes earlier. Well, this wouldn't do.

"I'd like to buy that last one," he told her. "And I'd like to have you autograph it as well, so I'll have a piece of you here with me after you've gone back to Atlanta." Something to hold him over until he saw her again.

"Actually," she said, setting the pens back down on the table and shifting the cookbook to hold out in front of her, "this copy's not for sale."

"It's not?"

Opening it, she turned the book around and held it out to him with a tender smile. "It's already yours."

Jake's gaze dropped to the handwritten words on the page in front of him. *To the wonderful man who helped make this cookbook a reality while stealing my heart in the process. You're the biggest part of my deciding to make Sweet Springs the town I call "home." Love you always, Addy.* Heart swelling, he looked up, meeting Addy's gaze. "You're moving here?"

She nodded, offering him the most beautiful smile he'd ever seen.

"Addy," he said as if she'd just taken his breath away, "there's so much I want to say." He was just reaching into the pocket of his jeans, prepared to take the biggest step of his life, when Addy spoke.

"Me first," she said, tears in her eyes. "I stand here today, living proof that dreams can change. Before this last visit to Sweet Springs, before spending time with you, realizing that I had loved you far longer than I even knew myself, I would have taken the country club's job offer without hesitation. But I've realized that wealth and security doesn't only come from the amount of money earned. It comes from being surrounded by those you care about. It comes in the ability to make time to enjoy the beauty of God's world. It comes from allowing yourself to take a chance on love and having that love returned."

Jake fought back a flood of emotion. Addy was his. The reason he'd survived the attack. She was, without a doubt, God's plan for him.

"Moving to Sweet Springs will make me far richer than I ever could have dreamed of being. In fact, I've already decided on a name for my new bakery, if your offer still stands— Sweet on You."

He wouldn't have thought it possible, but his heart swelled even more, joy filling it to near bursting. "It does. And you should consider yourself a very wealthy woman, Adeline Mitchell, because my love for you runs deeper than I ever thought possible."

"Oh, Jake," she sighed happily, a single tear slipping free to work its way down her cheek.

Smiling, he reached out to brush the drop of moisture away with his thumb. "I can't wait until Lila and Mason's wedding to walk my fiancée out onto the dance floor for our first slow dance together."

Addy's eyes widened. "What did you just say?"

Pulling the satin-lined box from the pocket of his jeans, he flipped it open.

A soft gasp left Addy's parted lips when she saw the ring nestled inside the tiny box.

Reaching out, Jake took her hand in his. "I would kneel before you if I were capable of doing so, but I'm not about to let a physical impediment keep me from laying my heart on the line. I treasure our friendship, but I want to be so much more than your friend. I want to be your husband. The man you turn to in your times of need. The man who will spend every day for the rest of his life doing his best to put a smile on your face. To protect you. To support you in all you do. And to grow in faith with you." Releasing her hand, he removed the ring from its satiny nest. "Addy Mitchell, will you marry me?"

Tears now flowing freely, she replied, "You don't have to kneel for me to know your words are heartfelt and your intentions true. And there's nothing I'd love more than to be your wife. In you, I've found my forever. The man I want by my side as I travel along the path the Lord has set me on."

"The man who is going to make your dreams come true," he promised.

"And I yours," she replied with a tender smile. "So, yes, Jake, I will most definitely marry you."

Cheers went up around the room. Moments later, Jake and Addy were surrounded by their families and closest friends, receiving well-wishes and hugs. He knew they had both faced darkness in their lives, but through love and faith they had found their way back to the light and to each other.

Epilogue

With the peach trees in full bloom, family and friends gathered for Mason and Lila's spring wedding, which was being held in the very place where they had first met—the orchard. The sun was shining, the sky a brilliant blue.

Addy stood at the makeshift altar next to Violet, watching as Finn, dressed in a miniature version of Jake's groomsman tux, escorted a radiant Lila down the aisle. The path strewn with pale peach rose petals looked nothing like the trodden-down ground over which they'd ridden ATVs.

"Who gives this woman to be married to this man?" Reverend Hutchins asked with a smile.

"I do," Finn piped up. "Daddy's marrying Momma, but he gets both of us."

The reverend nodded with a grin. "A very blessed man indeed."

Lila bent to give her son a hug and a kiss on the cheek before turning to face Mason. Finn moved to take his place between his daddy and Jake as they'd practiced the evening before.

Addy saw moisture fill Mason's eyes as he stood gazing down at his bride. Every person seated there in the orchard could see just by looking at them that Mason and Lila shared a deep, lasting love. At the thought of such an all-consuming bond, Addy's gaze moved past Mason to Jake, only to find him staring back at her. One side of his mouth quirked up into a slight smile. One she couldn't help but return. He was once again making good on his promise to make her smile every single day.

It wouldn't be long before she and Jake were the ones exchanging vows in front of their family and friends. Addy had sold her condo and, with her momma's blessing, had moved back to Sweet Springs shortly after Christmas. She was living with Mama Tully while she and Jake had begun plans for their own wedding. They had also gone together to purchase the empty building downtown, becoming partners in life and in love as they worked to make her dream a reality. In fact,

Lila and Mason's tiered wedding cake was the very first to be created at Sweet on You, Addy and Jake's wedding gift.

Once the vows were exchanged and Lila and Mason were pronounced husband and wife, the wedding party and all the guests moved to the yard in front of The Perfect Peach, where tables have been set up and meals were served.

"This day couldn't have been more perfect," Addy said to Lila as they feasted on the fried chicken and macaroni and cheese, which Finn, who had been placed in charge of the menu for the reception, had chosen. *Also perfect*, she thought to herself as she took another bite of Mama Tully's homemade macaroni and cheese.

"It was, wasn't it?" Lila sighed happily. "And to think that in less than a year you will be having your own special day with Jake."

"I know. I can't wait." She looked to Lila. "We'll not only be sisters of the heart, but sisters by marriage."

Lila smiled. "And we'll have Violet, too."

"Thank the Lord for blessing me with sisters," Violet, who was seated on the other side of Addy, said with a smile. "Sisters will finally outnumber brothers in the Landers family."

"Can't have that," Jake muttered from the other end of the table.

"Nope," Mason agreed as he bit into a crispy chicken leg. "Looks like we'll have to work on getting her married off so we can at least even out the numbers."

"Aunt Violet can marry Braden," Finn tossed out from the far end of the table.

Violet nearly choked on the drink of lemonade she'd just taken. "Aunt Violet is perfectly happy with her life just the way it is. Thank you very much."

Reverend Hutchins stepped over to the microphone. "It's time for the bridal dance. Would the new Mr. and Mrs. Landers please make your way out onto the dance floor?"

Addy watched as Mason took Lila's hand and walked her out to the dance floor he and Jake had built for events being held at the family orchard. Then Violet and Finn were called out to join them. Finally, Jake and Addy were asked to join the others on the dance floor.

His leg no longer in a cast, his shoulder completely healed, Jake stood and extended his hand. "This is the moment I've been waiting so long for."

Smiling, Addy slid her hand into his, their fingers threading as they crossed the yard to the dance floor. There, he drew her into his arms, the engagement ring he'd given her the evening of her book signing sparkling in the afternoon sunlight.

"You look beautiful," he told her as they moved in slow rhythm to the song Lila and Mason had chosen for this dance. "But then you always do."

Addy laughed softly. "You are quite the charmer, Jake Landers."

"I try my best."

Lifting her head from his shoulder, Addy looked up at Jake, a soft smile playing at her lips. "How is it when I think I've given you all of my heart I find out there's even more of it to give?"

"That's because love is limitless," he told her.

"I think happiness might be as well, because with each passing day spent with you, the happier I am."

"The best is yet to come, Addy girl," Jake replied, brushing a sweet kiss over her lips. "The best is yet to come."

* * * * *

Dear Reader,

Life isn't always storybook perfect, something Addy learned firsthand while growing up. While most of us have homes and families to comfort us, there are many who have little or nothing at all. They're forced to live in shelters or on the streets. That kind of life can make you strong or it can break you. Addy came out stronger and found happiness on the other side.

She did so thanks to the kindness of strangers, the support of friends she made along the way, and by the grace of God. So be kind to those less fortunate than you. Be it a smile, a helping hand, or a given opportunity to improve their life.

Jake's life took a turn that left him struggling with a shaken faith and deep-rooted guilt. He felt responsible for his friend's dying during the attack on his mission group. Those feelings pulled him into a dark place. He was able to work through the emotional trauma by opening up to Addy, reconnecting with his faith, and with his family's support.

While both Addy and Jake were able to find their way out of the darkness in *The Missionary's Purpose*, there is no shame in seeking professional help, be it through therapy, your pastor, or someone you trust. Only strength. And always remember to focus on your blessings, no matter how small.

Blessings,
Kat

Get 4 FREE REWARDS!

We'll send you 2 FREE Books
<u>plus</u> 2 FREE Mystery Gifts.

Love Inspired books feature uplifting stories where faith helps guide you through life's challenges and discover the promise of a new beginning.

FREE
Value Over
$20

YES! Please send me 2 FREE Love Inspired Romance novels and my 2 FREE mystery gifts (gifts are worth about $10 retail). After receiving them, if I don't wish to receive any more books, I can return the shipping statement marked "cancel." If I don't cancel, I will receive 6 brand-new novels every month and be billed just $5.24 each for the regular-print edition or $5.99 each for the larger-print edition in the U.S., or $5.74 each for the regular-print edition or $6.24 each for the larger-print edition in Canada. That's a savings of at least 13% off the cover price. It's quite a bargain! Shipping and handling is just 50¢ per book in the U.S. and $1.25 per book in Canada.* I understand that accepting the 2 free books and gifts places me under no obligation to buy anything. I can always return a shipment and cancel at any time. The free books and gifts are mine to keep no matter what I decide.

Choose one: ☐ **Love Inspired Romance Regular-Print** (105/305 IDN GNWC)   ☐ **Love Inspired Romance Larger-Print** (122/322 IDN GNWC)

Name (please print)

Address   Apt. #

City   State/Province   Zip/Postal Code

Email: Please check this box ☐ if you would like to receive newsletters and promotional emails from Harlequin Enterprises ULC and its affiliates. You can unsubscribe anytime.

Mail to the **Harlequin Reader Service:**
IN U.S.A.: P.O. Box 1341, Buffalo, NY 14240-8531
IN CANADA: P.O. Box 603, Fort Erie, Ontario L2A 5X3

Want to try 2 free books from another series! Call 1-800-873-8635 or visit www.ReaderService.com.

---

*Terms and prices subject to change without notice. Prices do not include sales taxes, which will be charged (if applicable) based on your state or country of residence. Canadian residents will be charged applicable taxes. Offer not valid in Quebec. This offer is limited to one order per household. Books received may not be as shown. Not valid for current subscribers to Love Inspired Romance books. All orders subject to approval. Credit or debit balances in a customer's account(s) may be offset by any other outstanding balance owed by or to the customer. Please allow 4 to 6 weeks for delivery. Offer available while quantities last.

Your Privacy—Your information is being collected by Harlequin Enterprises ULC, operating as Harlequin Reader Service. For a complete summary of the information we collect, how we use this information and to whom it is disclosed, please visit our privacy notice located at corporate.harlequin.com/privacy-notice. From time to time we may also exchange your personal information with reputable third parties. If you wish to opt out of this sharing of your personal information, please visit readerservice.com/consumerschoice or call 1-800-873-8635. **Notice to California Residents**—Under California law, you have specific rights to control and access your data. For more information on these rights and how to exercise them, visit corporate.harlequin.com/california-privacy.

LIR21R

Get 4 FREE REWARDS!

We'll send you 2 FREE Books plus 2 FREE Mystery Gifts.

Harlequin Heartwarming Larger-Print books will connect you to uplifting stories where the bonds of friendship, family and community unite.

FREE
Value Over
$20

YES! Please send me 2 FREE Harlequin Heartwarming Larger-Print novels and my 2 FREE mystery gifts (gifts worth about $10 retail). After receiving them, if I don't wish to receive any more books, I can return the shipping statement marked "cancel." If I don't cancel, I will receive 4 brand-new larger-print novels every month and be billed just $5.74 per book in the U.S. or $6.24 per book in Canada. That's a savings of at least 21% off the cover price. It's quite a bargain! Shipping and handling is just 50¢ per book in the U.S. and $1.25 per book in Canada.* I understand that accepting the 2 free books and gifts places me under no obligation to buy anything. I can always return a shipment and cancel at any time. The free books and gifts are mine to keep no matter what I decide.

161/361 HDN GNPZ

Name (please print)

Address   Apt. #

City   State/Province   Zip/Postal Code

Email: Please check this box ☐ if you would like to receive newsletters and promotional emails from Harlequin Enterprises ULC and its affiliates. You can unsubscribe anytime.

Mail to the **Harlequin Reader Service:**
IN U.S.A.: P.O. Box 1341, Buffalo, NY 14240-8531
IN CANADA: P.O. Box 603, Fort Erie, Ontario L2A 5X3

Want to try 2 free books from another series? Call 1-800-873-8635 or visit www.ReaderService.com.

*Terms and prices subject to change without notice. Prices do not include sales taxes, which will be charged (if applicable) based on your state or country of residence. Canadian residents will be charged applicable taxes. Offer not valid in Quebec. This offer is limited to one order per household. Books received may not be as shown. Not valid for current subscribers to Harlequin Heartwarming Larger-Print books. All orders subject to approval. Credit or debit balances in a customer's account(s) may be offset by any other outstanding balance owed by or to the customer. Please allow 4 to 6 weeks for delivery. Offer available while quantities last.

Your Privacy—Your information is being collected by Harlequin Enterprises ULC, operating as Harlequin Reader Service. For a complete summary of the information we collect, how we use this information and to whom it is disclosed, please visit our privacy notice located at corporate.harlequin.com/privacy-notice. From time to time we may also exchange your personal information with reputable third parties. If you wish to opt out of this sharing of your personal information, please visit readerservice.com/consumerschoice or call 1-800-873-8635. **Notice to California Residents**—Under California law, you have specific rights to control and access your data. For more information on these rights and how to exercise them, visit corporate.harlequin.com/california-privacy.

HW21R

HARLEQUIN SELECTS COLLECTION

From Robyn Carr to RaeAnne Thayne to Linda Lael Miller and Sherryl Woods we promise (actually, GUARANTEE!) each author in the Harlequin Selects collection has seen their name on the *New York Times* or *USA TODAY* bestseller lists!

YES! Please send me the **Harlequin Selects Collection**. This collection begins with 3 FREE books and 2 FREE gifts in the first shipment. Along with my 3 free books, I'll also get 4 more books from the Harlequin Selects Collection, which I may either return and owe nothing or keep for the low price of $24.14 U.S./$28.82 CAN. each plus $2.99 U.S./$7.49 CAN. for shipping and handling per shipment*.If I decide to continue, I will get 6 or 7 more books (about once a month for 7 months) but will only need to pay for 4. That means 2 or 3 books in every shipment will be FREE! If I decide to keep the entire collection, I'll have paid for only 32 books because 19 were FREE! I understand that accepting the 3 free books and gifts places me under no obligation to buy anything. I can always return a shipment and cancel at any time. My free books and gifts are mine to keep no matter what I decide.

☐ 262 HCN 5576   ☐ 462 HCN 5576

Name (please print)

Address   Apt. #

City   State/Province   Zip/Postal Code

> Mail to the **Harlequin Reader Service:**
> **IN U.S.A.:** P.O. Box 1341, Buffalo, NY 14240-8531
> **IN CANADA:** P.O. Box 603, Fort Erie, Ontario L2A 5X3

*Terms and prices subject to change without notice. Prices do not include sales taxes, which will be charged (if applicable) based on your state or country of residence. Canadian residents will be charged applicable taxes. Offer not valid in Quebec. All orders subject to approval. Credit or debit balances in a customer's account(s) may be offset by any other outstanding balance owed by or to the customer. Please allow 3 to 4 weeks for delivery. Offer available while quantities last. © 2020 Harlequin Enterprises ULC. ® and ™ are trademarks owned by Harlequin Enterprises ULC.

Your Privacy—Your information is being collected by Harlequin Enterprises ULC, operating as Harlequin Reader Service. To see how we collect and use this information visit https://corporate.harlequin.com/privacy-notice. From time to time we may also exchange your personal information with reputable third parties. If you wish to opt out of this sharing of your personal information, please visit www.readerservice.com/consumerschoice or call 1-800-873-8635. Notice to California Residents—Under California law, you have specific rights to control and access your data. For more information visit https://corporate.harlequin.com/california-privacy.

50BOOKHS22R

South Burlington
Public Library

COMING NEXT MONTH FROM
Love Inspired

AN UNEXPECTED AMISH HARVEST
The Amish of New Hope • by Carrie Lighte

When Susannah Peachy returns to her grandfather's potato farm to help out after her grandmother is injured, she's not ready to face Peter Lambright—the Amish bachelor who broke her heart. But she doesn't know his reason for ending things...and the truth could make all the difference for their future.

THE COWBOY'S AMISH HAVEN
by Pamela Desmond Wright

With three sisters to look after and her family ranch falling into foreclosure, Gail Schroder turns to her childhood sweetheart, Levi Wyse, to help her learn the cattle business. But can the cowboy teach this Amish spinster the ropes in time to save her home?

A MOTHER'S STRENGTH
Wander Canyon • by Allie Pleiter

Molly Kane will do anything to help her son overcome his anxieties—including enlisting Sawyer Bradshaw to give him golf lessons. But as the little boy draws them together, can Molly and Sawyer also heal each other's hearts?

LOST AND FOUND FAITH
by Laurel Blount

Changed by the grief of losing his wife, Neil Hamilton's no longer the caring teacher he once was—until a two-year-old boy shows up on his doorstep and opens his heart. Helping little Oliver bond with his adoptive mother, Maggie Byrne, might just restore Neil's faith...and give him hope for the future.

CHASING HER DREAM
by Jennifer Slattery

Returning home to run her late uncle's ranch, single mom Rheanna Stone never expected the operation to be in such disarray...or that she'd need to rely on the cowboy who once left her behind. But if she wants to save it, Dave Brewster's her only hope—even if it means risking her heart all over again.

THE BULL RIDER'S FRESH START
by Heidi McCahan

After former champion bull rider Landon Chambers's friends are killed in a car accident, the baby they were temporarily caring for needs him. But when Kelsey Sinclair returns from her deployment to claim her daughter, he's shocked to learn *he's* the father...and he's not ready to let either of them go.

LOOK FOR THESE AND OTHER LOVE INSPIRED BOOKS WHEREVER BOOKS ARE SOLD, INCLUDING MOST BOOKSTORES, SUPERMARKETS, DISCOUNT STORES AND DRUGSTORES.

LICNM0821